"There's Nothing To Say.

"Except that if I were you, I'd throw me off this boat. Think about it, Mick. It's good advice."

He tch-tched like a schoolmaster and held Kat close. He pressed her cheek against his chest and wrapped his arms tightly, securely around her.

Kat sighed. Mick had successfully reawakened lustfully active hormones she'd been praying were dead, dead, dead.

There was a wealth of masculine satisfaction in his voice when he said, "Kat, it's obvious that the problem isn't one *you* have to deal with. We have to work on this together."

"You're wrong," Kat protested.

"No, Kat. Remember you don't have a problem. We do. Because that's how it is when two people love each other. You *do* realize that you love me?"

Kat swallowed hard. His tone was light, but she knew he was serious. His heartbeat was thumping right under her cheek. How could she lie to him?

Dear Reader:

Sensual, compelling, emotional . . . these words all describe Silhouette Desire. If this is your first Desire, let me extend an invitation for you to sit back, kick off your shoes and enjoy. If you are a regular reader, you already know what awaits you—a wonderful love story!

A Silhouette Desire can encompass many varying moods and tones. The books can be deeply moving and dramatic, or charming and lighthearted. But no matter what, each and every one is a terrific romance written by and for today's women.

I know you'll love March's *Man of the Month*, *Rule Breaker* by Barbara Boswell. I'm very pleased and excited that Barbara is making her Silhouette Books debut with this sexy, tantalizing romance.

Naturally, I think *all* the March books are outstanding. So give into Desire . . . you'll be glad that you did!

All the best,

Lucia Macro
Senior Editor

JENNIFER GREENE

HEAT WAVE

SILHOUETTE *Desire*

Published by Silhouette Books New York

America's Publisher of Contemporary Romance

SILHOUETTE BOOKS
300 East 42nd St., New York, N.Y. 10017

ISBN: 0-373-05553-6

First Silhouette Books printing March 1990

Printed in the U.S.A.

JENNIFER GREENE

lives on a centennial farm near Lake Michigan with her husband and two children. Before writing full-time she worked as a personnel manager, counselor and teacher. Mid-1988 marked the publication of her twenty-fifth romance. She claims the critical ingredient to success is a compassionate, kind, patient, understanding husband—who can cook.

Her writing has won national awards from Romance Writers of America, *Romantic Times*, and *Affaire De Coeur*. She has also written under the pen name of Jeanne Grant.

One

Kat Bryant zipped into the driveway, braked her car with a jolt and grabbed the key to her spanking-red MG. The fast ride had destroyed her pompadour hairstyle. Her high-topped white button shoes hit the pavement, and when she climbed out of the car her lace-trimmed skirt slid down to midcalf. Customers regularly told her that the image of a proper Victorian lady suited her.

There were no customers around now, and the only thought in Kat's head was getting naked. Fast.

Damn, but it was hot. Charleston was always hot in July, but this summer's heat wave was a bone wilter. The sun blistered and anything green had long ago been bleached white. The birds were too parched to sing; everyone was cranky, and there was no escaping the susurrant drone of air conditioners. Even at five in the afternoon, the temperature sustained a choking hundred degrees.

Kat made a beeline for the shade, not hard to find in a neighborhood where most of the houses were three stories tall. Her home, like all the rest, was built right off the street with French-style shutters and wrought-iron balconies. A history lover would see the ambience that was old Charleston. The more practical would note the lack of parking, the internal layout of small rooms and long, inconvenient stairs. Kat, a sucker for history, had taken one look at the house five years before and passionately fallen in love.

At the moment, however, she was only feeling passionately about heat. Her workday had stretched to twelve frazzling, wilty, sticky hours. She'd been good—as good as the girl with the curl in the nursery rhyme—but enough was enough.

The very instant she got inside, she planned to throw the dead bolts, strip to the buff and pour herself a wickedly long, dripping-cold glass of lemonade. She'd drink it stark naked, and she could already taste it. She could also already picture herself decadently immersed in a cool scented bath, preferably with ice cubes, and definitely with the phone off the hook and no interruptions. Maybe she'd even eat dinner in the bathtub. Who'd know? Who'd care?

No one, and that was the real luxury. She fumbled in her oversize bag for her house key. After this sweltering day, all she craved was an evening of peace and solitude. Cool, silent peace, stressless solitude ...

"Hi, Kat!"

"Hi, Kat! You're home late!"

Her fantasy, especially the parts involving decadence, nudity and solitude, popped the moment she saw the two teenagers clattering down her porch steps. Mick Larson's girls had obviously been waiting for her to come home—and not for the first time.

Kat felt the buck of frustration, but not for long. The two girls gamboling toward her with their hopeful smiles inevitably tugged at her heart. Angie, at thirteen, was a classic waif. She wore her blond hair crimped Shirley-Temple style, and her slight frame was voluminously hidden in one of her father's shirts—attire chosen, Kat guessed, to hide any hint of newly developing breasts.

Mick's oldest daughter Noel could have used a little of her sister's shyness. She was fifteen and looked ready to hook from the nearest street corner. Her favorite color was unrelieved black. Today her black shorts and tank top were set off by three earrings per ear and her short brown hair was well spiked with mousse. If Kat squinted hard, she could see the beautiful pair of eyes hidden beneath layers and *layers* of mascara.

"Hi, sweeties." Kat turned the key in the lock and stepped aside. Not that they were sure of their welcome, but the girls pelted in faster than puppies in a rain. "Your dad have to work late again?"

"Dad's got a big important job," Angie told her.

"I'm sure he does." There was no rancor in Kat's tone, but the look of the girls made her think briefly and fondly of homicide. She loved the girls. It was their father who deserved a good bludgeoning.

Mick Larson had been burying himself in "big important jobs" since his wife had died two years ago. The whole world had loved June—she'd been a naturally earthy woman with a heart bigger than the sky—

and when she'd died, the whole neighborhood had tried to comfort Mick in his grief.

Kat hadn't known her next-door neighbor well enough to comfort him. Not that he was unfriendly, but the brawny Norwegian had never been easy around her, and that uneasiness was definitely mutual. She'd tried to help by spending some time with his daughters, but that was like plugging a small finger into a fast-growing hole in a dike.

One of these days, Mick Larson simply had to wake up and smell the coffee: both his girls were running wild and lonely, thanks to his neglect. Angie needed a bra. Noel modeled her makeup techniques after Madonna. Both skipped school in winter and throughout the summer had filled the house with a steady stream of kids. Noel was running around with a turkey who drove a Hell's Angels type of motorcycle, and Angie . . .

"Could I have something to eat, Kat? We don't have *anything* in our refrigerator. There is nothing to eat in the whole house."

"As if you needed to ask. Go on, sweetie, help yourself. You know where everything is." Still in the hall, Kat grabbed a button hook for her old-fashioned shoes. It took a full two minutes to wriggle her toes from their cramped confinement. That should have improved her mood. It didn't. The situation was clearly getting progressively worse next door. Now Mick didn't even have food for them to eat.

Noel returned with a tall glass of lemonade in her hand—the same lemonade Kat would have given her eyeteeth for. "Your outfit's spectacular," she said admiringly. "You really look terrific."

"Thanks, honey." Kat's tone was wry. Noel's compliment lacked some validity since the fifteen-year-old's concept of fashion would have nicely fit in with the motorcycle crowd.

"Kat, I just want you to know...if we're in your way, we could go home."

Never mind all the heavy makeup, Noel's expression was so unsure, so vulnerable. Damn that man, Kat thought again. "You two are *never* in my way," she said swiftly. "If you hadn't come over, I'd have been stuck with a long boring evening with no one to talk to."

"You sure?"

"Positive." Kat might not be a cook, but she could put together a trayful of cheeses and fruits. The girls dived into the snack like vultures...or children who hadn't been fed in a year.

"You're sure you don't have something to do? Like a date or something?" Angie asked.

"Not tonight." Once she'd glanced at the mail and put away the tray, Kat headed for the stairs, trailed by both sidekicks.

"You should date more," Noel advised her sagely.

"Hmmm."

"I'll bet good-looking guys ask you out all the time."

"Hmmm." Since Noel's life revolved around the male of the species, Kat could hardly tell her that she hadn't dated in years. Five years, to be precise.

Rather than dwell on the enforced loneliness of her single life-style, she chose to see her situation with humor. She was saving a lot of men a lot of potential grief by removing herself from the dating market.

Humor didn't always save her from loneliness, but Kat wasn't about to let a man close again. It wasn't a question of once burned, twice shy, or any other hang-up that some expensive psychologist could help her with. She had a problem, all right—an intimate, personal problem—but there was no solution for it. She'd faced that because she had to and gone on with her life. But *her* problems, at the moment, were the last thing on her mind.

Upstairs, Noel draped herself on the bed with such wanton abandon that Kat had to smile. "I love this room. It has to be the most romantic room in the entire world."

"You think so?" Plucking at her blouse buttons, Kat spared her bedroom a whimsical glance. French doors led onto the second-story balcony. Two narrow stained-glass windows framed the small marble fireplace. Light filtered through the stained glass, casting prisms of rose and blue on the blue carpet, the antique "sleigh" bed and her collection of Victorian hatboxes in the corner. From the dozen lace pillows piled on the bed to the hatboxes, the room was a study in old-fashioned femininity... barring the pair of strappy red shoes with four-inch heels peeking out of the closet, which Kat quickly kicked out of the girls' sight.

Her house advertised a very solid dose of feminine values, but there were other things—such as her high-speed sports car, and her red strappy high heels—that might give someone the idea she was a classic rule breaker. With June gone, the girls had no feminine role model. Kat did her best, but the job was tricky. She knew zip about raising kids, and both girls were insatiably curious.

Too curious. She deliberately ducked behind the closet door before stripping off her long-sleeved blouse, but that bid for privacy was wasted. Noel and Angie simply relocated where they could see her.

There was nothing wrong with changing clothes in front of the girls. It was just that men in a singles' bar couldn't possibly study a woman with more critical bluntness than a teenage girl.

The spray of freckles on her shoulders was judged with the same gravity as the band around her waist left by her panty hose. Kat whipped on a pair of white shorts, because Noel was staring at her wispy panties with a frown. She chose a brief yellow top in deference to the heat, but made a point of wearing a bra beneath it in deference to Angie's unrelenting study of her breasts.

"When I'm as old as you are, I wouldn't mind a figure like yours," Angie mentioned.

"Thanks."

"But I'll bet the boys stare at you. I'd die if a boy stared at me. Especially there."

Kat only had to look at Angie to remember how painful it had been to be thirteen. "Luckily boys aren't all that fascinated in an ancient old woman of thirty-three," she murmured.

"You're not really that old, are you, Kat?"

Kat chuckled. "Afraid so."

"Well, don't worry about it. You're still beautiful," Noel reassured her protectively. "My thighs are so fat; you think I should diet? Oh, this is *wonderful*. You really wear this?"

Kat gently confiscated the black silk nightgown from Noel's avid fingers and dropped it in the back of her closet with the red shoes. "Occasionally, and no,

I don't think you should diet. I think you look just fine the way you are."

"These are French panties, aren't they? Tap pants? I suppose you think I'm too young to wear stuff like this?"

Kat was rapidly developing a headache, which matched up to her parched throat and increasingly frazzled nerves. She had definite opinions about what Noel should and shouldn't wear, but there was an enormous difference between acting as an occasional feminine influence for the girls and interfering. How Mick raised his daughters was his business, not hers. She wanted no business at all with Mick Larson...but how long was she supposed to stand by and watch the girls suffer from his indifference and neglect?

She tried to erase the man from her mind, but that was easier said than done. Both girls trailed her into the bathroom. While she washed her face, they interrupted each other with an insatiable stream of feminine chatter. What was the best cover for zits, how old was she when she first shaved her legs, what kind of curfew did she have as a teenager? Not every question was emotionally loaded, but each implied a lack of guidance in their lives. Dammit, Mick, how can you be so blind?

Normally her bathroom did a reasonable job of distracting them. The black marble tub and lemon tiles were a style out of another century. Angie had a fascination with the old-fashioned pull chain on the toilet. Noel loved to touch the silver boudoir brushes and lemon soap. Today, though, they were simply more interested in talk—and watching Kat convert an elegant pompadour hairstyle into a ragamuffin top knot.

Her long, dark auburn hair was her pride and joy, when the temperature was fifty degrees. In this heat, she was inclined to shave her head . . . either before or after she shaved a strip off the girls' father.

"I did all the wash today," Angie reported.

"So what's to brag? I did all the vacuuming and washed the kitchen floor. Dad makes a total mess when he tries to clean the house," Noel confided. "Men are so helpless. I was going to shop for some food, but he forgot to leave me money this morning."

Kat set down the hairbrush with a snap. A week before, Angie had described making a pitiful dinner out of nacho chips slathered with peanut butter. That was bad enough, but the more Kat heard about the enormous household responsibilities each girl claimed, the more she was tempted to strangle her next-door neighbor. What killed her most was that the girls never complained. Ask them, and their father was a combination of Rambo, Robert Redford and a knight in shining armor.

"You think this perfume is too strong for me?" Noel asked.

"Which one, honey?" Since Noel had sampled most of the vials, the narrow bathroom was starting to reek like an expensive bordello. One scent had no prayer of being distinguished from another.

"This one. You think Johnny would think it was sexy?"

"I . . . ummm . . ." Abruptly Kat headed for the door. Downstairs she could turn on the TV. Surely the news would provide some nice, innocuous earthshaking disaster they could discuss.

"What's a douche, Kat?"

"Pardon?" Kat stopped midstride on the top stair.

Angie, standing in her usual hunched-over position designed to hide her new figure, repeated patiently, "What's a douche?"

Noel loomed behind her sister, creating a traffic jam at the top of the stairs. "I told you what a douche was," Noel said irritably. "I told you all that stuff a long time ago."

"Yeah, well, you told me if I kissed a boy I'd get AIDS. I saw you kissing Johnny and you didn't get any AIDS. Anyway, the last thing I'd want to do is kiss some stupid old boy. I just want to know what a douche is."

"Well, it's..." Kat cleared her throat, and then blessed the girls with her best calm, serene smile. Well? How are you going to answer that one, ducky? an inner voice taunted her. The thing was, there was a huge difference between discussing zits and discussing douches—and the Lord only knew what sex education Noel had passed onto her younger sister. Darn you, Mick Larson...

"I'll answer that question, okay? Just as soon as I pour a lemonade downstairs. I'm dying of thirst."

"Don't worry about it, Kat." Noel said to her younger sister, "I've told you a zillion times not to bother Kathryn with questions like that. All you have to do is come to me."

"Yeah, well, I came to you, and I'm still not all that sure you know what it is."

"I do, too. When a woman gets to be a certain age, she automatically knows these things, don't we, Kat?" To Angie she snapped, "I told you. A douche is sort of like a tampon." She hesitated. "I think."

There were headaches and then there were headaches. This one was accelerating to magnificent proportions. "We'll talk about it, okay? Just as soon as I pour that lemonade." Kat said gaily.

Around midnight, Kat gave up trying to sleep and carried a glass of sherry outside to the porch steps.

It was still hot. Moonlight shimmered in the honeysuckle and flickered through the branches of the gnarled cypress at the far end of the yard. Lightning bugs played in the cache of wild roses sprawling over the back fence. Dew had settled in the grass, thick and fragrant.

Leaning against a porch post, Kat took a sip from her glass and grimaced. There was nothing more nauseatingly sweet than cooking sherry. She liked an occasional glass of good wine. She just never remembered to buy it.

Like a child with medicine, she forced another gulp. She'd counted on the wine to make her sleepy. It wasn't working. She'd counted on the fresh air to relax her. That wasn't working, either. Scarlett O'Hara would have enjoyed a southern summer night like this: the crescent moon, the mingled scents of honeysuckle and roses. But romance was a forbidden subject for Kat. Normally she had the willpower to walk away from trouble.

Over a very long evening, though, she'd discovered that she couldn't buy or beg enough willpower to stop worrying about the girls.

She took another sip of sherry, yet suddenly couldn't swallow it. In the next yard, she heard the unmistakable slam of a screen door. The lights in the Larson house had been out for almost an hour, but someone was up.

Mick. Moonlight shone on his silver-blond head for only seconds before he moved into the shadows. She heard the creak of a lounge chair, then the pop of a can top.

She still hadn't swallowed the gulp of sherry. When she did, it burned all the way down her throat like liquid fire. All evening she had decided to talk to him if the chance presented itself. Unfortunately the ideal chance had just presented itself. He was alone, the girls were asleep and no one was around to interrupt them.

Nerves coiled in her stomach as she slugged down the last of the sherry and firmly set down the glass. She had never meddled before, never intruded in anyone's private affairs. It took some courage to break those long-standing principles, but if she didn't talk to Mick, who would? Sure he'd be ticked off. So what? June would have been appalled to see her daughters neglected, and it wasn't as if Kat didn't have some tact. She wasn't going to go over there and call him a selfish, insensitive, unfeeling rat.

She was just going to go over there and wish him a neighborly hello. And then clobber him, she thought darkly.

Dew soaked her bare feet before she was halfway to the fence. The sticky grass tickled, but not half as much as the sticky situation she was about to take on.

Southern women, however, had always been made of good strong grit. Kat firmly reminded herself of the girls' voracious, starving raid on her refrigerator, their woeful tale of endless household chores, their hunger for attention and, yes, the douches. She reached the fence, fueled by cooking sherry and unshakable resolve.

"Evening," she sang out with the determination of an advancing general.

He was stretched out in the shadows, but she saw his silver-blond head swivel in her direction. "Evening, Kathryn," he called out in return.

"Finally cooled off a little."

"Not much."

"Scheduled to be another scorcher tomorrow."

"So they say."

She leaned on the white wooden fence rail and remembered, much too late, that she'd never managed more than conversational drivel with Mick Larson.

For five years, she'd felt incomprehensibly, aggravatingly awkward anywhere near him. It had never made sense. Maybe she dressed in lace and cameos, but she could climb a ladder and put up a Lincrusta frieze as capably as a construction crew. She liked men, she knew them, she worked with them. And it was never as if Mick had been rude or cruel or unfriendly toward her. The opposite was true. On the rare occasions their paths crossed, he had always treated her carefully, as if he was never quite sure if the lady would bite.

Kat had stalked over with every intention of attacking his conscience, but—with more brilliant hindsight—it was a very bad idea. Six foot three of brawny muscle was slowly swinging out of the lounge chair and ambling toward her. She was a respectable five feet, six inches . . . in heels. His dwarfing shadow made mincemeat out of her visions of clobbering him, and something was going equally wrong with her visions of Mick as a selfish, insensitive rat.

She knew what the girls had told her, but the man leaning his elbows on the fence rail just didn't look like an insensitive child neglecter. He looked tired.

Actually he looked exhausted. How many weeks had it been since she'd really had a look at him? Moonlight played up the clean, strong lines of his face, but she could still see the dark shadows beneath his eyes. He'd put in a hard, physical day in the heat and it showed.

June had once told her his age, but Kat had forgotten. Thirty-seven, thirty-eight? His body didn't look thirty-eight. He wasn't wearing a shirt, and his arms and shoulders had a fighter's roped muscles, tanned to a dark, dark copper. Faded jeans hugged his spare hips and hard, powerful thighs. His thick, rumpled hair might have been a natural wheat color. The sun had bleached it to a white gold, and his chest was dusted with that same striking white.

He wasn't pretty, but no woman was likely to ignore him in a crowd. His square face was the map of a man's values. Sun-squint lines were permanently embedded around his eyes; laughter lines bracketed his mouth. He worked hard and he played hard; he had the jaw of a boss and the furrowed brow of a man who'd wrestled with life on his own terms. No desk job or wine lists for Mick. He was a physical, earthy, sexual being in the most elemental sense: he never forgot he was a man.

Kat would have liked to. Like a certain kind of uncommonly large man, he walked with a cat's silence and had a gentleness about him. A sleek, long rifle had power, but not until someone cocked the gun. Dynamite was dangerous, but not until it was lit. Mick had never done anything to appear intimidating.

But he was. This close, Kat's stomach felt the aggravating drip, drip, drip of nerves. By daylight, his eyes were a brazen cerulean blue. Now they were immutably dark and so intently focused on her that her bare toes arched in the dirt of the flower bed bordering the fence. A mosquito landed on the back of her calf. She let it bite.

"You don't have to hesitate," he said gently. "We're neighbors and you're living alone. I've told you before you could call me anytime."

"Pardon?"

"You have a leaky faucet? An appliance on the fritz?"

"I . . . no."

One of his sunburned brows arched in question. "You don't stop to talk to me very often. I figured something had to be wrong."

"There is something," she agreed.

His voice was low and as alluring as the darkness and scent of roses. He didn't mean it that way, she knew. If Mick was coming on to a woman, she'd know it. It wasn't his fault his voice was sexy. It wasn't his fault her darn toes were curling. "How's the yacht-building business going?"

"Too busy," he admitted, and then offered, "You've been good to my girls. They talk about you all the time. I'm long overdue on a thank-you."

"Yes? Well . . ." If her right foot curled any tighter, she was going to get a charley horse in the arch. She took a long breath, smiled at him and said blithely, "I'd like to talk to you about them for a minute, if you wouldn't mind."

"About my daughters? Anytime."

Again, she had the sensation that something was drastically wrong with the image of Mick as an uncaring father. Still, she took a breath and forged ahead. "Dammit, Mick, Angie needs a bra."

He blinked. "Beg your pardon?"

It all spilled out faster than bad news. "And I know it's not my business, but if it were *my* daughter, I'd be meeting that Johnny at the door with a shotgun. Damnation, Noel isn't my daughter but I'm inclined to go take rifle practice. And I think responsibilities are wonderful, but all the cooking and washing and cleaning is just too much. And then there's sex. If you can't talk to them comfortably, you could buy them some books—accurate books—or at *least* make sure you know where they're getting their information. It's not that I mind discussing the facts of life with them; I just feel it's something I can't do without your permission. How do I know what you want them to know? And food. Who likes cooking? But you could still stock your refrigerator with sound, nutritional munchies. Not just chips. And Noel's talking about putting another hole in her ear—"

"Could we hold up two shakes?" Mick interrupted peaceably.

At the moment Kat couldn't. It had been too hard to start, she couldn't stop now. "I know this is none of my business. You probably think I'm a meddling, interfering pain. You have every right to raise your daughters exactly as you please, but Mick, they're so lonesome for attention. And they have to have guidance. At the very least, you simply have to remember to give Noel money for food—"

"Kathryn?"

"Noel told Angie that a girl 'can't get pregnant the first time.' I'm going crazy! They don't know anything and they're passing on the wrong stuff to each other—"

"Kathryn—"

"I understand you build boats to make a living, but would the world cave in if you built a few less? Who needs steak? Go for hamburger. I know grief isn't simple; I know June was absolutely wonderful, but your daughters are still alive, Mick. Right now Angie's entire wardrobe appears to be your shirts—"

"Kat!"

"They're too *young* for the entire responsibility of the household! Please don't be angry, but—"

"I'm not angry."

Silence fingered through the night, as quiet as a heartbeat. "Of course you're angry," Kat assured him.

"No."

More silence. "You must be." Her own temper was kept under strict wraps, but if anyone tried to nose in her private life, Kat knew darn well she'd have unsheathed every claw and come out spitting. She was so prepared for a tongue-lashing that his slow, crooked smile left her grappling.

"No. A part of me feels kicked in the seat, which maybe needed to happen. And a part of me feels amused."

"Amused?"

Mick nodded. "My angels, my daughters, those two beings I love more than life who live with me...I think they just took you for a ride."

"A ride?"

He nodded again. "It's pretty obvious you've formed an opinion of me as a man lower than a worm, a father who's lost total interest or concern for his children and who deserves a long, slow hanging. But could you possibly hold up the lynch mob long enough to come inside the house? Just for a few minutes. It won't take long to show you that, just possibly, there's another side to the story."

Two

Mick had to coax her to come inside. He knew she really didn't want to. He also wasn't in the habit of explaining or defending himself to anyone, but this was different. The idea that anyone would believe he'd neglect his daughters hit him low and hard.

At the gut level.

The kitchen was dark. He switched on the overhead light and immediately strode over to the refrigerator. The kitchen was pine and white, nothing fancy, but at least the counters were clean, which his next-door neighbor immediately noticed. He noticed the awkward way she stalled in the doorway. "I won't traipse through your house, Mick. I was standing in the flower beds; I'm afraid my feet are really dirty—"

"It won't be the first time the floor's seen a little dirt. Besides, we have a housekeeper."

That took her attention. "Housekeeper? But the girls said—"

"Maybe housekeeper's the wrong word. I have a lady who comes in three mornings a week to tackle the cleaning and wash."

Kat drew a breath. "But Angie said—"

"Yeah, you gave me a good idea what Angie told you. Would you mind taking a peek in here?"

She tiptoed, with very small, very dirty feet, over to his open refrigerator. She glanced at him once, wrapped her arms tightly under her chest and then bent down to view the inside shelves. They were bulging. Fresh fruits, fresh dairy products, sliced meats, cheeses, vegetables...

"I..." She scratched an itch on the back of her calf and then straightened. Her spine could have made a functioning straight edge and her lips compressed, but an interesting coral was beginning to skate up her throat. "Sooo..." She drew out the syllable as if she was stuck pulling taffy. "It's pretty obvious the girls aren't starving."

"Lord, I hope not. You should see my grocery bill."

"And don't tell me," she said weakly. "Noel doesn't do all of the family grocery shopping."

"Hey, she's the best shopper in the family, as long as you're talking about clothes on my credit card. Unfortunately when you get down to the nitty-gritty of eggs and toothpaste, her interest gets real rocky." Mick suddenly realized he was staring at Kat, seeing her differently than he had before, aware of her toast-brown eyes, her long bare legs, her nerves. Reacting to those nerves, he crouched down and squinted in the refrigerator again. "Noel's not the only one who hates grocery stores. I never claimed to be a master shopper," he drawled. "You see anything in here that looks poisonous that I didn't realize?"

Kat was swallowing hard and frequently. "Mick, I'm sorry, and I—"

"Could you come here, please?" He closed the refrigerator, opened the door to the broom closet and turned around. "Really. Would you just take a quick glance inside?"

"It's a broom closet."

"I know. Just look, okay?"

With the patience of one obliging a madman, she obediently moved closer to him and peered inside. For that brief moment, she was so close that he caught the drift of perfume on her warm skin, the scent of her hair. His pulse bucked, startling him.

He busied himself moving a box of the usual household cleaning supplies from the top shelf. The tall box, once removed, hid a cache of potato chips, chocolate bars and fruit gummies. "Angie changes her lair from week to week," he said matter-of-factly. "From the time I forbade junk food in the house, she became a hoarder. I hate to tell you what I found last fall in my fishing hat in the front hall closet."

"Tell me."

"Hardened toffee, jujubes hard and stale enough to break your teeth, and six-month-old Hershey Kisses." Mick's eyes glinted down at her. "Do you have any idea what a summer season of heat can do to a Hershey Kiss?"

Kat didn't laugh outright, but he heard her chuckle…and he saw the chuckle fade into a soft, shy woman's smile. Again, he felt an unexpected tug, a bolt of sexual awareness.

She obviously didn't. Mick didn't need a degree in perception to realize that she was fast changing her mind about what kind of father he was, but that didn't mean she had made up her mind about him as a man. He motioned her to a bar stool across the counter and pulled a beer from the fridge, asking if she wanted one. She shook her head, then nodded.

Before she could change her mind again, he set the beer in front of her, then hefted a can for himself, which he didn't want any more than she did. Flipping the lid gave him something to do, so did removing the draftsman sepias from the Formica counter and settling on the bar stool across from her.

They were talking again before he'd finished all that inane busywork. In those spare seconds of silence, though, Mick was dominantly aware that a woman hadn't been in his kitchen in a long time. And that, of all the women who might have been there, the last one he'd ever imagined was Kat.

Kat—née Kathryn—Bryant confounded him, always had. With the exception of June, Mick had never been good around women. Kat had the ability to make him feel huge, awkward, and vaguely, annoyingly panicked.

He'd never figured out what to make of her. She dressed in lace and old-fashioned hats, but she also tore through the streets in her sassy MG. She carried a purse big enough to store a machine gun, yet the girls told him she had a carousel horse in her living room. She had the look of a fragile camellia, yet three years ago he'd seen her patching her roof, shingle by shingle, alone. And competently.

She was not only competent, but a sound business woman. She'd spent the past five years building up a

Victorian restoration business—Victorian was "in," so she sure didn't lack competition—but she'd made a serious name for herself. Mick felt both respect and empathy for what she'd achieved, but he'd never been able to express that. Frankly her looks intimidated him.

Take her hair. The color was sort of a rusty cinnamon. Undone, it reached halfway down her back. Mick had seen it undone. He'd also seen it in a strange-looking pompadour, he'd seen it sleeked flat to her scalp and he'd seen it wild with curls. She changed the style all the time, how was a man supposed to figure out who she was? One day she looked like a schoolmarm virgin, the next day she looked like a vamp.

All of the time she looked like an unusually desirable woman, which, given the whole picture, confused Mick even more.

Kat was smaller than two-bits, but even in old shorts and a saggy yellow top, she was a dynamo. Her light brown eyes were full of life and humor, intelligence and passion. She always moved lithe and quick and light, like a breeze wisping by, like a streak of light and sparkle. Maybe she wasn't beautiful, but the rich auburn hair, fine bones and delicate cream skin would capture any man's attention. She had a way of walking that said she loved being a woman and she flaunted that fact to the whole darn world.

Only that feminine flaunting was precisely what confused him, because Mick had never seen her with a man. His daughters said men called, they'd heard the telephone calls during the hundred and ten times they visited her in a week. But no date's car showed up in her driveway on the weekends. She was home all night, every night. Mick had been her next-door neighbor for five years. He knew.

And that was one unbelievably long time for an attractive woman to be totally alone.

Of course, it was an equally long time for Mick to discover that she wasn't so bewildering or intimidating. In fact, she was turning into someone impossibly easy to talk to.

"I'm not going to criticize your daughters to your face," she promised him. "I'd just like your permission to privately strangle them tomorrow, if you don't mind."

"Maybe we could form a line?"

Her finger followed a droplet of water racing down the cold beer can. She still hadn't opened it. "Now that I think about it, I can't believe how blindly I believed them. The 'poor me' stories never added up. They both glow every time they say your name, hardly a symptom of neglected children. All I can say is that I love your girls, and I felt protective about them, and I didn't and don't really know you. Anyway, I owe you a giant apology."

"No, you don't." It finally occurred to him that he should have given her a glass. Restlessly he surged to his feet, produced the glass, popped her beer top and poured it in. "If my girls hit you for sympathy, maybe it was because they needed it," he admitted gruffly. "I'm guilty of not spending enough time with them. Maybe I'm guilty of worse than that. You already know I build boats—"

"Yes."

"And there are a lot of boat builders in the business, but very few craftsmen who only work in wood, which is to say that I have unlimited business if I want it. Two years ago, I wanted unlimited business. I wanted so much work I couldn't breathe, sleep, eat or think. So I went after it, and I got it.''

He motioned with his hand, a man's gesture, the closest he had ever come to admitting helplessness. ''It's not that I didn't think of Noel and Angie, but they seemed okay. The three of us had had two years to prepare for June's death; at the end that was a blessing more than a shock. And they seemed to be doing better than I was; they seemed to be taking it all maturely. They weren't, and aren't, mature, but by the time I realized things were going wrong, I was up to my neck in building contracts.''

''You don't have to explain all this to me,'' she said softly.

But he did. He needed to explain it to someone. And the woman sitting across from him, with her knuckles curled under her chin and her soft eyes, was listening. Mick could remember others willing to listen, but not anyone where he'd felt the willingness or need to share. ''Months ago, I started getting out from under. I hired help and I eased off on taking new contracts, only I couldn't make it all happen overnight. You have a business of your own—''

''I understand,'' she concurred.

He knew she did, although most independent businessmen that he knew didn't have tobacco-brown eyes and a mouth so fragile it worried him. ''Anyway, I've done what I can to get out from under, only to discover that normal working hours didn't solve anything. Kat—'' he took a gulp of beer ''—I'm scared.''

''Scared?'' she echoed. She deliberately raised herself from the bar stool to take a meandering perusal of his linebacker's shoulders and muscular long legs.

Another woman could have done the same thing and made it into something suggestive and sexual. Kat's eyes pounced back to his with simple, easy humor. She'd noticed he was a big lug of a man, but she hadn't noticed he was a *man*.

Mick felt piqued. "Scared," he repeated determinedly.

"It has to be a lot of years since bogeymen in the closet intimidated you, and something tells me you don't often wake up with nightmares."

"Would you cut it out? I'm serious. I'm scared of them."

"Them?"

"Them. My daughters. Noel. Angie."

She'd finally relaxed enough to take a sip of beer, and now she nearly choked on it. "Are you crazy, Mick? They adore you. They worship the ground you walk on."

"That's what I'm trying to tell you. As a father, I'm walking into quicksand. I'm not just talking fear, I'm talking panic. I got lost months ago somewhere between permanents, sanitary napkins, tight jeans, makeup and dating rules of the '90s." He hesitated, aware of the faint streak of color on her cheeks. "Did I offend you? I know Noel has a stroke if I mention a feminine product out loud, but it seems pretty silly for a grown man to pretend he's unaware that a woman..."

"I'm a little older than Noel. Trust me, I can handle the conversation."

She could and she was, but the flush climbing her face definitely fascinated him. The redhead had a secret Victorian streak. Mick hadn't known there was a woman alive who was still modest. And with those sassy eyes?

"Where I was raised, a man called a spade a spade. I never had a polite education in euphemisms. My whole family were men, which is undoubtedly why I end up in such hot water all the time."

"Hot water?"

"With my daughters. I thought I could handle raising the girls through puberty. That was a mistake." He heaved a sigh of the long suffering, just to catch another of her grins. "For instance, a few months ago, I *thought* I was showing some honest sensitivity in buying Noel some Midol. I mean, there was no ignoring it. Once a month she was—"

"A little moody?"

"A little moody?" Mick said patiently, "You looked at her, she cried. You talked to her, she cried. Ask her if she wanted a glass of milk, and she stormed out of the room and slammed the door. A few days later and she was back to being Noel, but in the meantime—"

"I understand."

"Do you? Because I swear to God I've tried, but I don't. More relevant, if you can understand that stuff, maybe you can understand the phone."

"The phone?" Kat queried gently.

"Yes. The phone. In a fire, there'd be no getting a call through to this house. Both girls live on the phone; they do their hair, the dishes, their homework and even their nail painting on the phone. I mean, is this something unique to the female genes? Is there a cure? And darn it, will you quit laughing?"

"I'm not laughing."

"Close enough," he grumbled, but the sparkle in her eyes pleased him, delighted him. So did she. He was close enough to catch her scent and it wasn't French and fancy like he'd first thought. It was something cool and light and innocent, like Lily of the Valley. The woman had too much devil in her eyes to wear Lily of the Valley, but he was beginning to feel more intrigued than intimidated by the many contradictions that made up Kat. How could he have lived next door to her for five years and never heard her really laugh?

So he kept on. "This fathering business used to be a lot of fun. When they were younger, we'd traipse off to Hunting Island for the weekend to beachcomb and fish. Never needed more than a knapsack apiece and some food. Now it takes Noel forty-seven suitcases, most of them packed with electrical appliances, before she'll ever...you're not laughing again, are you?"

"No. I promise. No."

"And they've both turned sneaky. They never used to be sneaky. They used to be just people. Little people, maybe, but definitely recognizable as the human species. Noel asked me if she could have some earrings, and I said sure. Next thing I know her ears look like pin cushions. Was I supposed to say no?"

"Well, pierced earrings *are* the fashion."

"Is showing her fanny the fashion? Because she tells me it is. How am I supposed to know? Every friend she brings in looks just like her—horrible. I haven't seen her eyes in a year. I think she wears that gunk to bed, and I keep thinking I should be drawing the line. Only where exactly is this famous line? She brings home all A's. Her teachers think she's a peach. I don't see how a kid can develop judgment if you don't give her some leeway, some trust, some freedom. And I do trust her." Mick clawed a hand through his hair. "At least I think I trust her. I know I used to."

Kat's slim white hand closed on his calloused one. The contact was as brief and simple as the empathy she needed to express. "I know these issues aren't easy, and they're even tougher because you're a single parent, but don't you think it's possible you're handling it all better than you think?"

"If I was handling it all that well, Kat, I doubt they'd have hit on you for sympathy." His voice was gruff edged. She'd quickly lifted her hand, yet he could still feel that pampering softness.

"And I've been thinking about that." Her eyes reflected honesty. "I don't think what Angie and Noel did was so unusual, so terrible. Maybe you were a nice adolescent? I was your average total pain, spent half my time groaning about how rough I had it at home. I had it great at home, but it was much more fun to share war stories. Complaining is just something that kids do."

"Maybe they've had reason to complain—"

"And maybe you're too tough on yourself."

"I don't think so. We used to be able to talk together. Suddenly I don't know anything and my opinion is worthless—"

She had to smile again. "Mick, they love you. The worst stuff is all going to pass."

"Never." His tone was spiced with humor. "I'll never be able to make a business telephone call at night for the next sixty years, because believe me they'll never leave home; they'll never marry. Any guy in his right mind who ever takes one look in the girls' downstairs bathroom and..." Mick suddenly stiffened. "And who was this *Johnny* you mentioned?"

Kat started to answer and then checked herself. "Ask Noel."

"In other words, you're not telling?" He murmured, "I'll kill the boy. I take it he's wild?"

"Ask Noel," she repeated with a chuckle.

"I'm asking you. To help me." He didn't know where those words came from, but suddenly they were out. "Not for problems, Kat. I'm not looking for anyone to solve my problems, but there are times I'd really appreciate the chance to talk, get some advice. Some *female* advice."

She shook her head quickly. Too quickly. "I'm the last person you should ask. I not only don't have any kids, but have never been around any. My opinion's worth zip."

"But you're a woman. And they dote on every word you say. They both quote you every time I turn around. You have to be better at some of this stuff than I am."

She looked at him in a way he didn't understand. One minute there was dance in her eyes, a warmth so natural it could make a man's pulse race, and then it was gone. She glanced at the wall clock and sprang off the stool. "Good grief, did you realize how long we've been talking? It's after one. I have to work tomorrow and so do you!"

Even though he was on his feet, she still reached the door before he did. As quickly as she obviously wanted to escape, though, she suddenly hesitated. "Mick, I really think you're asking the wrong person, but if you want some help—at least to a point—you know I'm next door. I can't imagine that you would feel comfortable bra shopping with Angie. There's no reason I couldn't do that, and I'd be glad to.''

"Fine," Mick said, although suddenly nothing was. He opened the door, and she said some platitude about being glad they'd talked together. She'd turned back into a stranger. True, in a sense they'd never been more than strangers, but he'd felt something more that night, something special, something real—something that had mattered a great deal to him.

He wanted to tell her that she'd been warmth and brightness on a night that would have been bleakly lonely without her—but he didn't know how to say it.

Because he didn't know any other way to express a thank-you, he leaned down, slowly, closer. She didn't bolt when she felt the graze of his lips. She simply froze like a fawn startled by lightning—which perplexed him. He couldn't possibly threaten her; Mick never threatened women. Kat may have ignited his senses all evening, but he'd already banked any hint of sexuality or excitement because she obviously didn't feel the return pull. A kiss of thank-you was all he intended, all he delivered. His mouth covered hers, so tenderly she couldn't possibly misunderstand, so briefly he had only the promise of the taste of her, and then he lifted his head.

That's all that was supposed to happen. Maybe that's all that would have happened ... if her sable-lashed brown eyes hadn't suddenly lifted, if her fingers hadn't clamped hard on his wrists. He read all the "no" messages, but she didn't move. She just kept looking at him until the air charged with a sweet, humming tension. It took him a moment to understand.

Kathryn had so much breezy confidence she could intimidate a man without half trying.

Kat didn't.

Kathryn had control of her emotions down to a science.

Kat—this Kat, with the soft, bleak, fawn-brown eyes—couldn't always.

They were still standing in the open door. Air conditioning blasted them on one side. The night heat blasted them on the other. For a moment that was how it felt to him, as though they were caught between the chill of loneliness and the alluring dark promise of heat.

He crossed the threshold. Cupping her chin, he angled her face more securely. The pulse in her throat caromed at the stroke of his thumb. She tried to shake her head, which struck him as wise. Her skin was far too soft for the caress of his rough callused palm, and it had been so long that he wasn't sure he remembered how to do this.

Silken strands of cinnamon shimmered through his fingers as his head dipped down. He abruptly discovered that no previous memories were going to help him. Kissing Kat would never be like kissing anyone else.

So still. She went so still. He didn't take her mouth, just sipped, tasted, savored. And then covered it as gently as a whisper. There it was again—the sensation that he was strength to her fragility—but the taste and texture and scent of her went to his head. The illogical thought occurred to him that he hadn't missed a woman in all this time. He'd missed Kat.

And her small lips, so immobile, suddenly came to life under his. Her hands unlocked from his wrists and

moved, climbing his arms, not like a temptress playing some teasing game but like a woman, so slowly,
coming alive. Tongues touched, both dry, and then
neither was dry and he drew her to him.

She shuddered, hard, when her small breasts made
the first contact with his bare chest. Temptation, dark
and desperate, had the feel of her arms locking hard
around his neck. Her mouth yielded under his, not in
willingness but in yearning.

Mick only knew hunger from a man's point of view.
A man could live without fire. He could toughen
himself against cold; he could live in darkness if he
had to; he could talk himself out of need. He could do
all that for a long time. But not forever.

He knew those things as a man, but had never
imagined them from a woman's point of view. Kat's
hunger was as raw, as wild, as scared...as innocence.

He kept telling himself that she was crushably small,
to be careful...careful. Yet his hands chased down her
slim spine to her even slimmer hips. He cupped her
closer. He kissed her until he couldn't breathe. And
then he kissed her again, because he didn't care about
breathing.

She'd confused him for so long, and still did. But
not now. He could taste her loneliness like he could
taste his own; he could sense her wariness, her fear, yet
her mouth still moved under his, searching, seeking.
Not sex. This need was far darker, far more dangerous than sex. Sometimes you just had to know there
was someone else out there, even if it was only for a
moment, an instant, a crashing brief second of time.
You had to believe there could be someone who
understood, someone you could touch.

The rush speeding through him nearly shattered his conscience, yet he felt shock dart through her, her sudden stiffening. She broke free first. Or she tried.

He understood she wanted to pull away, and that was fine. But not like that. Not like teenagers, embarrassed, jumping away from each other.

He wrapped his arms tighter around her, just for another moment until her frantic breathing eased and quieted. He smelled roses, heard the whisper of a night wind, let his fingers slide in the silk of her hair. He kissed her forehead. A kiss of comfort.

"It's all right," he said gently, which was the only way he knew how to say relax. Neither had intended that dark, hurling abyss of heat, neither had expected it. He would never have forced it further, she didn't have to be afraid. Not of him.

But it wasn't all right, not for her. She bolted back as soon as he freed her. Her skin was flushed, her mouth trembling. "I didn't—"

"Come on, Red. Take it easy, neither did I."

"I don't know what—"

"Neither do I."

"It was just a mistake. People sometimes make mistakes. But you can trust me, Mick, it won't happen again."

She was gone, pelting barefoot down his back steps and blending into the night shadows before he could respond. He didn't know what he would have said. Her comment had been like an apology. Since he'd sure as heck been guilty of initiating the embrace, it didn't make much sense.

But that didn't surprise him. He had never understood Kat.

He waited until he saw her fly up her porch steps, heard the whack of her screen door close and watched her porch light flick off before returning inside.

Perhaps it was past one in the morning, but any chance he'd had of sleep had just been destroyed. He poured the beer from both full cans down the drain, turned off the lights in the living room and headed upstairs to check on the girls. They were both sleeping. Noel had the radio on, Angie had a ragged stuffed elephant tucked next to her pillow. He turned off the radio, retucked the elephant, and ambled to the third floor upstairs—and the nearest west window.

Her house wasn't identical to his, but most of the old homes in this "French" block of Charleston had been built at the same time. Downstairs, he had a kitchen, utility, dining and living room. The second floor had two bedrooms and a bath. The third floor had a single room, arched under the eaves.

Kat's house was similar in layout; she simply used her rooms differently. Mick slept on the third floor. In her house, Kat slept on the second. Her bedroom light burned for another half hour. Even after she turned it off, he found himself still standing in the window, staring down at the moonlight shining on the lace curtains of her bedroom.

His didn't have lace. He had functional polyester-cotton curtains of some indeterminable bland color. No furnishings in the house showed any fuss. June had never shown an interest in decorating.

His wife, so unlike Kat, had been a woman that a man could be easy with. There had been nothing fragile about June in size or character. She'd been boisterous, earthy, natural. She could swear harder than he could, hammer a nail with equal skill, and—

until her illness—their love life had been lusty, physical and frequent. She'd never called him for a flat tire. She'd fixed it herself. And she had borne their daughters alone, because June very honestly hadn't wanted or needed him there.

Mick had never accommodated his life-style for his wife, not because he hadn't been willing, but because June would have been angry if he'd tried. There were men's men. June had been a man's woman, independent and in control and strong.

The two years of slowly debilitating illness had destroyed her spirit. People thought he grieved at her death, which wasn't true. He'd done all his grieving during those two long years. June had hated living through them, and Mick had felt a failure for being unable to help her, to matter to her, to be the someone who could make a difference through the pain. Wasn't that what a husband should be?

Mick had loved her, there was no question of that. But there had always been something missing—not for her, but for him. June had never needed him. As a man, as her husband, as simply another human being, Mick had needed to help her, especially through those last rough months. She'd never given him the chance.

When she died, people had misunderstood his workaholic obsession as grief. Guilt was the real reason he'd buried himself in work. Physical exhaustion was far easier than the nag of wrong memories. June had been perfectly happy until her illness. Lord knew he had every reason to feel the same. He couldn't possibly have married a finer woman. June was good, clear through to the bone.

It was a fault in *him*. He'd been married to a very good woman for fourteen years...and he'd been as lonely as hell.

He turned away from the view of Kat's window. Stripping down to the buff, he dropped onto the muslin sheets and turned out the light.

Kat was not June.

She was nothing like June.

Maybe she had the independence and the pride, but she was also nuts. She wore hundred-year-old clothes and yet flashed through town with that wild red hair. And she came on to a man with need, a need so naked and tangible that it had taken his breath away.

It was still taking his breath away.

Sometime, somewhere, somehow he'd hoped to matter to someone. Maybe he'd stopped believing he could because of June, and Kat...it had to be a mistake to mess with a woman he didn't understand. It would be a worse mistake to risk hurting someone who'd already been hurt.

He didn't, of course, know if Kat had been hurt. The late night, the heat and a too-long period of celibacy could have colored his perception. The lady herself was a distraction. Her perfume. Her small-boned body layered against his, her tiny tight breasts, a pelvis like an erotic cradle, the taste of her....

You know how much work you have tomorrow? You're not going to get any sleep if you don't hang it up, Larson.

But for the first time in months, maybe years, Mick didn't want to sleep.

Three

I understand you want a bracket. But are you talking scross, quarter circle, gothic...?'' Hunching over to cradle the phone between her ear and shoulder, Kat scribbled down the order. When the door opened to her miniscule office, she was still talking.

Georgia, dressed in Victorian garb from her whalebone corset to her bustle, mouthed a single word: "Help."

Kat grinned, severed the phone conversation as quickly as she could and strode through the door of the boutique. At lunch there hadn't been a handful of customers. Now there was a herd of them. Kat's assistant, Georgia, was thirty-nine, a curly-haired brunette with a cultured drawl and a fatal attraction to jam cookies. She looked as if she'd never handled any tougher decision than the day's choice of shoes, but both women knew who really ran the antique boutique. It wasn't Kat. Georgia didn't need a posse, she was the posse, but she also knew Kat needed a break from the blasted telephone.

Two shoppers were porcelain doll collectors. Kat handled them first, then aimed for the three white-haired ladies hovering over the jewelry counter. "Miss Bryant! Last week you had a garnet ring in this case, a stone surrounded by seed pearls. There was an inscription."

"I remember. You'd like to see it again?"

The rosy-cheeked matron wanted to look, not buy, but Kat didn't mind. Throughout the discussion of antique jewelry, her gaze drifted possessively around the store.

The whole place was filled with scents and sights designed to woo and charm the antique buff. Nothing was rigidly displayed. Kat was too smart to organize: customers loved to hunt, loved to feel they'd uncovered "a find." Shelves, open drawers and even the floor had been sneakily planted with "discoveries"— an 1890s harp, a rocking horse, glass-bottomed lamps and stained glass, high-button boots, skeins of lace, sterling spoons and doll houses.

For those customers who failed to succumb to visual stimulus, Kat had done her best to attack their noses. She sold sachets and soap, and the scents of oranges and cinnamon, roses and lemon and chamomile had long since invaded the store. If their noses didn't lead them to a sale, Kat delivered a third and more ruthless assault on the more vulnerable part of a woman's body: her stomach.

Some stores had a pot of coffee for their customers. Kat had a pot of wassail, or of tea. While a customer sank into the wicker cushioned love seats to wile away an hour, she was treated to a meringue kiss, or a jam cookie, or—when Georgia had time—a shamefully delicious bite of Princess cake. Fresh Victorian baked items, naturally, were available for sale at the cash register.

The three white-haired ladies wandered away. Two more customers popped in. Kat could tell at a glance that neither was dying to part with their cash. She loved the shop, everything in it and everything about it, but before her first month in business had been up she'd known that boutique profits were never going to keep her rolling in jellybeans.

Georgia motioned her to grab a cup of tea and scat, and Kat would have aimed back toward some real work if the bell hadn't tinkled yet another time.

Mick strode in faster than a barreling bull, but then he stopped dead with a comical panicked look on his face. Every woman in the store glanced up at him. He wasn't naked, but the feeling of embarrassment must have been similar. Few men walked in there wearing worn jeans, dusty work boots and carrying a hard hat. His T-shirt was a respecable white, but his shoulders were bigger than most of Kat's aisles, and unless he breathed very carefully he was about to knock down a cascade of lace shawls.

Georgia, outstanding at averting disasters, abandoned the cash register and rushed toward him. She stopped, thoughtfully, when she realized the stranger had spotted and recognized Kat.

Mick's eyes fastened on her as if she were water and he were thirst. It was the same look he'd given her three nights ago, just before she'd come to her senses and escaped from an embrace that should never have happened.

There was something dangerous about Mick, and it wasn't that he was about to topple two dozen shawls. The danger in Mick was the boyish save-me grin, the cocky tilt to his shoulders, the steady dark blue in his eyes as he watched her walk toward him. Damn him, she couldn't help chuckling any more than she could stop the aggravating sizzle in her pulse at his nearness.

"Don't breathe, don't blink, don't move," she ordered him.

"Believe me, I won't."

She saved the shawls and flashed him a cheeky grin. "If you'll shrink about five inches and tuck in your elbows, I think we can get you through the store. My office is in back." Her smile faded as she searched his face. "It had to be pretty serious for you to interrupt your workday. What happened?"

"Pardon?"

"You must have come to talk about a problem with Noel or Angie?"

He hesitated. "Yes."

So, she thought, he *hadn't* come about the girls. Mick may build big yachts, but he had a serious problem delivering small lies. He was honest to a fault, a fact she'd discovered three nights ago, which was why, possibly, she'd lost her head at the time. Mick was a good man, the kind of man any woman could justify losing her head over for a few lost, beguiling, heart-stopping moments . . . unless that woman was Kat.

His gaze dawdled over her hair, swept up with old-fashioned ringlets, her demure high-necked blouse pinned with a cameo, her powdered nose. His lips twitched. "It always intimidated me," he murmured.

"What did?"

"The look of the touch-me-not, eternal virgin. And I don't think you dress for the customers, Red, but because you have a heck of a lot of fun with it."

The way he said "Red"—bourbon warm and lazy—sent a slew of tickles down her spine, which she abruptly straightened. The obvious thing to do was herd Nick into her office, on her turf, where she would have better control of a friendly, innocuous and outstandingly quick conversation.

The plan was good. It just didn't work. Georgia headed for Mick with a handful of meringue cookies. Georgia saw a man, she fed him. And Mick, with the fascination of someone who'd landed on a foreign planet, couldn't seem to walk two feet without pausing to cautiously examine something on the shelves or floor. When he finally stopped dawdling, Ed, Kat's fuzzy-haired "retired" carpenter, hustled in from the back with a shipment he wanted her to check.

"I won't be a minute, Mick."

"I can entertain myself. Don't worry about me."

But she was worried about him. She wanted it settled—why he was here, what he wanted. Unfortunately there was no time. Her cramped boutique had once housed a restaurant, but the back was as big as the warehouse it was. Ceiling fans couldn't budge the South Carolina humidity out here. Sun streamed onto the loading dock; heat shimmered on the yellow-nosed forklift. As fast as Kat handled Ed's problem, the phone rang and then a truck arrived.

She saw Mick wandering around, but she couldn't stop the flow of interruptions to catch up with him. Tendrils of hair started curling damply at her nape—maybe from heat, maybe from nerves—yet the customers kept cornering her, not Ed. If they wanted a

Doric pedestal sink, she had it. If they wanted a span-drel or a Chippendale door or a gooseneck faucet, if they wanted to cost out a total renovation or see samples of porch balusters, they all knew Kat was the lady with the sharpest pencil. Ed knew the business, but he couldn't supply a strap-butt iron latch that hadn't been manufactured in this century. Kat would find the antique latch if she had to travel to Boston, and that kind of perseverance had built her reputation. A woman did what she had to do. Maybe antiques were her love, but the sweat and reality of renovation construction was where she made her living.

Every time she craned her head, Mick's sky-blue eyes were fixed on her like a scientist enjoying his research project . . . or like a man putting the puzzle pieces of a woman together. Kat was short with a customer—she was *never* short with a customer—and then she lost sight of Mick altogether.

By the time the distractions disappeared, she was frazzled, sticky and hot, and she found Mick happily hunkered down over a box of tin ceiling medallions.

He may have been cautious and wary in the crowded domain of her antique store, but her warehouse was obviously another story. She doubted Mick ever played hooky on a workday, yet he showed no inclination to hurry. His gaze was charged with curiosity and interest—a man's interest—and not for the tin ceiling medallions. His eyes never left her face as he slowly straightened. "Is it always this busy?"

There now. They could talk about business. "I wish," she said dryly. "This summer's been the best I've ever had. Everyone's in a hurry to fix up their houses this year, and thank the Lord, history is 'in.'"

"High overhead?"

"Horrible. My grandmother originally staked me in the antiques, but I couldn't make a profit up front to save my life. The only reason I keep them is that I love 'em ... and I delude myself into believing that the antique-buying customers are natural leads for the bread-and-butter business back here."

"You're making it?"

"So I've convinced the bank. For the past three years, they've—suspiciously—agreed that I'm a solvent enterprise."

Humor—or empathy—made him smile. "It's a lot for one person to manage."

She shook her head. "Not really. I have help coming out of my ears. There's Georgia up front, and a couple of part-timers. Ed works the back, he'd be here in a hurricane. We hire out the custom work, so there are several outside crews—plumbers, carpenters, construction. Most of the time I have nothing to do but sit in my office and look lazy."

"Kat?"

"Hmmm?"

Mick's cool blue eyes met hers over the rim of a lemonade glass. "You couldn't look lazy if you tried. But could you try to relax? I didn't come here to bite."

She didn't specifically remember him steering her into her office or him pouring the glass of lemonade he was holding. One minute they were outside and she was bubbling about her business, a brilliantly safe subject. The next minute Mick seemed to be installed, and sprawled, in her only spare office chair.

Georgia had obviously unplugged her phone—no one else but her assistant would have had the nerve. It was the first time Georgia had ever overtly tried to interfere in her private life.

Georgia, of course, had no real concept of what her private life was about. Kat did, which was why her pulse was skittering. Her office's air conditioning never functioned well on a day this hot. The room was overly warm, and Mick was close. He smelled like sunshine and wood and a man's warm skin. He smelled... physical. And he hadn't come here to talk about balcony balusters.

"Mick..." She twisted a napkin around the cold lemonade glass and then set it down on her over-crowded desk. Every time she looked at him, she was reminded of a man spilling out his heart because he loved his daughters. Every time she looked at him, she saw a very rare breed of very good man, and dammit, he made her pulse race. That pulse had to settle down because Kat was an old friend with the painfulness of honesty. "If you're here, by any remote chance, because of what happened the other night..."

Mick, the same Mick who'd always shared a matching case of nerves around her, indolently crossed his ankles. "I don't remember anything that happened the other night," he said mildly. "At least nothing that should be making either one of us nervous... or anxious. Do you?"

"No." She repeated cheerfully, "No, not at all. So, you really did come here to talk about the girls?"

He waited a split second, considering her over another swallow of lemonade. Eventually, though, his drawl obediently picked up the topic of Noel. "I met her Johnny two days ago—a meeting I seemed to have handled with the finesse of a Mack truck. Noel has since told me, several times, that she's no longer speaking to me for as long as she lives."

Kat couldn't help a smile, this time a natural one. "Poor Mick."

"During one of the times she 'wasn't talking to me,' we ventured into a dangerous discussion of dating habits in the 1990s." Mick scratched his chin. "Habits she made clear I know absolutely nothing about. People don't date anymore, I gather?"

In spite of his lazy drawl, she felt a prickle of uneasiness. Or was it awareness? "If you're asking me—I'm afraid I'm a long way from being an authority on the subject."

"No? Somehow I'd counted on you to be the one woman I could talk about this with."

"I'm not saying we can't talk about it—"

"Good." He watched her try to unobtrusively fumble with the phone cord and connection. She wanted that phone plugged in like a flyer wanted a functioning parachute—just in case. "Need some help there?"

"No, no." She dropped the cord faster than a hot potato, grabbed her lemonade glass and smiled. "Go on about Noel," she encouraged.

"My problem is complicated. See, when I was entering the dating scene in the '70s, sexual freedom was in." Mick cleared his throat. "Now it's obviously out. Noel has definite plans to be a virgin when she marries. I clearly misjudged her, and probably offended her for life. I thought I was being realistic and understanding. I had no idea women had given up all feelings of sexual desire these days."

The devilish man looked at her with those honest, guileless blue eyes. She could have swatted him. Three nights before, Mick had made it clear that sex was as comfortable a topic for him as Red Sox scores. She couldn't argue with that. Theoretically, two mature adults should be able to rationally discuss any subject on earth, only there was a level where theory broke down for Kat. There was a level where he was touching some private, murky waters that had nothing to do with his daughter, and she kept having the nasty intuition that he knew it.

"My daughter gave me quite a lecture on AIDS. And condoms." Again Mick cleared his throat. "I have to say that I wasn't quite prepared to have a discussion with my fifteen-year-old daughter on current birth control/safe-sex practices."

"Mick—"

"She knows more than I do. I'm a thirty-seven-year-old man. You think that wasn't humiliating?"

Darn him, she had to chuckle. The sound appeared to captivate him because his gaze was riveted to her mouth but only for the space of a heartbeat. When their eyes met, she lost another heartbeat, and then he forged on, gently, slowly.

"I literally haven't dated in years, Kat . . . which my daughter was quick to point out. How can I make rules for her when I don't have the least idea how to woo, seduce or even talk to a woman on '90s terms? Noel thinks I need coaching."

"Mick—"

"I think I probably need a heck of a lot more than coaching. Even years ago, I was never good at romance, never had a polished technique or knew the right words like some men. There was a time I knew how to show a woman I was interested, but any skill gets rusty when it's been locked in storage." He leveled her a cocky grin. "Of course, if a very understanding woman with a hatful of patience was willing to offer me advice . . .''

Odd, how parched her throat was. "We are, naturally, talking about advice you want for Noel."

Both of Mick's shaggy brows arched. "What else could we possibly have been talking about all this time?" He reached for his hard hat and stood up. "And just having the chance to spill all that out . . . it helped. More than you know."

She hadn't done a thing to help him with Noel, which he knew—and she knew—and he knew she knew. Shaking off that kind of shambled reasoning, she surged to her feet. "You need to get back to work?"

"Yes, and besides, I've taken enough of your time."

"I'll guide you through the store—"

"No sweat, I'll take the back way out. I confess that when I first walked in the front, I was good and lost and very sure I was going to bungle something."

She saw him smile. She also saw him bend down and turn his head. She had time to duck; it just never occurred to her that he was going to kiss her until it was already done. His lips barely touched hers. His fingers barely grazed her cheek. Her stomach barely had time to drop clear through the floor.

Then he leaned back and reached for the doorknob. "I just thought we'd both be more comfortable knowing the other night was a fluke," he murmured. "There really wasn't anything to be nervous or anxious about. Right, Red?"

"Right."

"Yeah." He grinned, jammed on his hard hat and closed the door behind him.

Kat sank in her office chair and slid her hands through her hair, dislodging pins and ringlets and not caring. That man! Either her imagination was working overtime, or Mick Larson was one of the most upsettingly perceptive men she'd ever met.

He claimed to have been talking about his daughter, but it was Kat who'd felt nervous and anxious about those first night's kisses. Kat who hadn't dated in years. Kat who'd put all sexual feelings in permanent cold storage.

Her office door opened. Kat jerked her head up. It was only Georgia, come to collect the tray of lemonade and glasses. "A hundred and seventy-five in the till—sold the red glass-bottomed lamp. How about that?"

"Terrific," Kat said.

"Quiet as a tomb out there now. I'm going to send Marie home early."

"Fine." Kat waited, certain Georgia was going to say something about Mick. In the five years they'd worked together, both had formed a unique bond of friendship. Most women talked; they didn't.

Respect and caring could sometimes be measured in silence. Kat had long guessed that a man was the painful subject in Georgia's background, but she never asked, just as Georgia had always refrained from advice or comment on Kat's private life—until this afternoon. How long had she and Mick been out in the warehouse? Not long. Georgia must have scrambled faster than a track sprinter to set up the lemonade and disconnect her telephone.

But now Georgia said nothing about the miracle surprise of her having a personal visit from a man. She just smiled and swept up the tray. "Don't ever be afraid I can't hold down the fort if you want to leave early sometime.''

''I won't be leaving early, Georgia.''

''There now. You sound jumpy. I swear the heat's getting to everybody,'' her assistant said mildly, and left.

Kat reconnected the phone and spent the next hour shuffling through the pile of receipts and work orders, thinking that Georgia was right. The heat wave was the problem. There hadn't been rain in weeks, just that endless blasted sun and humidity. A person couldn't think in this kind of heat. You couldn't escape it, couldn't ignore it, could never quite get it out of your mind.

He's a good man, Kathryn. A special man. And you like him.

When the pencil broke in her hands, she picked up another. *Yes,* she liked him. He was strong and big and gentle. He had a sense of humor, a natural way about him, and she'd been so wrong about what kind of father he was! Love reeked from him every time he talked about his daughters. He was trying so hard to be a good father. He was human enough to own up to his mistakes.

And he made her pulse quicken like no man, no where, no how, ever had.

The paper in front of her eyes blurred. She gave up trying to concentrate and rubbed her temples hard. The word frigid popped into her mind. A woman could be frigid in different ways. She could fail to feel desire. She could get hung up on inhibitions so a climax was impossible. Or, for whatever reasons, she could just be too afraid to let go.

Only the neat, handy label of frigid didn't work for Kat. Fear of men or sex had never been her problem. She found it shamefully easy to be turned on—with the right man. She wanted and needed to be loved—not just physically but in every way—and she knew her body was capable of a climax.

With a man, that experience simply caused her pain. Real, unignorable, physical pain. And in bed—in a nice darkened room with the lights off and two people on fire with need—pain was one hell of a thing to surprise a man with.

She'd die before ever putting another man through that again.

The phone jangled. She let it ring.

Kat might be celibate, but she wasn't naive. Mick wouldn't have come here if he hadn't been interested . . . and so was she. Mick had buried himself in work for so long. No matter how much he'd loved June, he had to realize that he was still alive, still a man with needs and emotions that needed sharing. He might as well have said that a woman would need a hatful of patience to take him on, and such honest vulnerability had touched Kat. Mick didn't need anyone's patience. The right woman could easily coax him out of his shell.

Well, that sure as sweet patooties isn't you, Kathryn.

She'd help him with his daughters, but otherwise she simply had no choice but to stay totally out of his way.

At the dot of two on Saturday, Kat locked her door and headed down the steps with her suitcase-size purse in one hand and a list in the other. She had to adjust both to push on a pair of sunglasses. The thin metallic red frames matched the straps on her flat sandals, and her white shirt and shorts were as cool as she could get without going naked. She'd wound her hair into two braids worn at the top of her head, but the sun still beat down at a baking 103 degrees.

Ignoring her own car, she crossed the pavement to Mick's driveway just as Angie slammed the screen door. "Did you remember your dad's car keys, honey?" she called out cheerfully.

"Noel's bringing them."

Kat glanced up from the list in her hand, startled at first by the child's downbeat tone, and second by the moody, miserable look in her eyes. "What's wrong?" An hour before Angie had been on top of the world.

"Everything. This is about to turn into one of the worst days in my entire life."

"Sweetheart, I thought you were looking forward to going shopping together. There's no reason on earth we have to do this if you don't want to."

"I do, I do. But I wanted to go with just you. We can't shop for the you-know-what now. Please, Kat, don't even bring it up. Please!"

"Angie—"

Noel interrupted them when she clattered down the Larson porch steps. She was predictably dressed like fifteen going on thirty-three and that included many layers of mascara. She dangled Mick's car keys in her hand. Because Kat's MG only seated two, Mick had volunteered his T-bird for the girls' shopping expedition. The last Kat knew, both girls had been delighted at the prospect. One look and she could see Noel's exasperated expression matched her sister's. "He's coming. We have to wait for him," she said with the weariness of the long-suffering.

Kat was totally confused. "Who's coming?"

"Dad."

"Since when is your *dad* coming with us?"

"Since he decided a half an hour ago that he felt guilty for copping out." Noel puckered her heavily glossed lips at the reflection of the car window, then sighed. "That's what he thinks. That he's copping out. Because he doesn't know anything about girls clothes and stuff. So he says it's about time he learned, and we don't have to worry because he won't say a word. He'll just trail behind you as quiet as a mouse."

Angie made a sound in her throat like the newly wounded. "Kat, can't you talk to him? I mean, we don't want to hurt his feelings, but couldn't you tell him that he can't come?"

Kat felt the brief sensation of being swallowed in quicksand. She'd have put on makeup and dressed differently if she'd known Mick was coming. Or, more likely, she wouldn't have dressed at all, because there'd have been no outing if she'd known Mick was coming.

He'd been calling her every night—only for advice on his daughters—but those rambling night calls and his low, throaty voice had had a nasty effect on her blood pressure. She'd done a rotten job of cutting those calls short, but that didn't mean she wanted to see him. Avoidance might not be the better part of valor, but it sure felt safer.

Unfortunately that was not necessarily an attitude she wanted to project to his daughters. "I can't quite imagine anyone telling your father not to do something, especially me," she admitted wryly. "Anyway, we're making too much of this. It won't be that bad."

"Oh, it'll be that bad," Noel assured her morosely. "You don't know Dad in a store. He doesn't shop. He *hates* shopping, and the worst part of it is that he thinks he has to do this to help us.''

''You know what he said?'' Angie moaned. '' 'Everyone wears underwear. Boys. Girls. Everyone, so what's there to be embarrassed about?' I'm going to die.''

The screen door slammed yet a third time. For a brief moment Mick didn't seem to see his daughters. He only had eyes for Kat. It only took seconds for fire to chase down a match stick. Mick's gaze, bluer than the baking-hot sky, took it all in—the braids, the sun burning on her bare legs, the no makeup, the shorts as white as innocence. Unlike Noel, Kat looked thirty-three going on fifteen, but he didn't look at her as if he saw a child. The way he looked at her made Kat feel like a sexy desirable woman. He made her feel . . . nervous. His slow smile didn't help.

Eventually he pushed on a pair of sunglasses and focused his full attention on his daughters. That quickly, Kat could have sworn the temperature dropped back down to a manageable 103 degrees. The sunshine stopped feeling electrified, and abruptly Mick didn't look any different than any other father about to suffer the tortures of the damned.

Slowly he ambled toward the car. His chin was freshly shaved, and he'd apparently nicked his throat. He was wearing khaki cotton pants, a freshly creased shirt and a propped-on smile. And his whole demeanor reminded her of a man striding for the noose. ''Gee, a whole afternoon of shopping,'' he said heartily. ''Won't we have fun?''

Four

At ten o'clock that night, Kat was in her backyard, lying prostrate in a lounge chair. Her eyes were closed, her zest was zapped, her nerves were shot. She had an arm thrown over her eyes to block the moonlight. A neighbor's cat was stalking through her honeysuckle. She didn't pay attention. It was hotter than Hades, but she didn't care.

She heard the back door open next door. She never budged. Even when she heard the creak of wood caused by an extremely strong man leaning on the fence, she never raised an eyelid.

"I thought it went pretty well, didn't you?"

His voice was very low, very sexy, very virile, and as hopeful as an anxious child's. It took Kat a moment to find the strength to speak. "Get over here, Larson."

She heard the latch on the gate. "I mean, sure, it took me a little time to get into the sizes and styles and

whatever. Why does girls' stuff have to be so complicated? But after that—''

"*Sit.*" She pointed one finger downward.

Obediently he sprawled out on the grass near her
feet. He hadn't bothered with a shirt, and he sighed—
a rich, lazy sigh—when his bare back sank into the
cool, night-dewed grass. Masculine contentment
reeked from him, even when she leveled him her most
severe scowl. "You and I," she said flatly, "are about
to have a little talk about the differences between girls
and boys."

"Sounds like fun, but it shouldn't take too long. I
already know I have a whatchamacallit and you
don't."

"This is a more important difference."

"I had no idea there was one," he murmured.

She gathered the last threads of her stamina, and
leaned over to pluck enough grass to throw at him.
The tiny green spears speckled his chest. He didn't
remove them, just grinned.

"Try and pay attention," she told him. "The *real*
difference between girls and boys begins at the doors
to a shopping mall. *Any* shopping mall."

"Come on, admit it. I did pretty good with the girls.
I didn't hold any of you back, did I?"

Kat opened her mouth, but her voice failed her.
He'd been awful. There was no other word for it. They
hadn't been in the first store twenty minutes before
he'd started asking, "Are we about through?"

It wasn't that he hadn't tried, but he shopped like a
primitive hunter stalking game. Noel had picked up a
sweatshirt with spangles on it. That was it, he was off,
scouting out anything in the whole damn store that

had spangles, and never mind if it was size two, ten, or forty-four. "How about this, Noel?" he'd asked.

By mistake, he'd walked into a dressing room. By mistake, they'd allowed him in the earring store. He'd stood with his hands on his hips and a terrible frown. "So... we're looking for pink, are we?"

The girls had kept looking at her. Do something with him, Kathryn, their expressions had said. Lord knows she'd tried. She'd managed to take him aside and firmly explain that he was not going with them to the lingerie section, also that he wasn't to make one comment or take *one* look at Angie when they came out. Mick had gravely deferred to her judgment. He hadn't taken one look at his daughter. In fact, he'd nearly mowed down his youngest in a doorway because he was carefully focusing above her head.

The man would still be at the panty-hose counter if Kat hadn't saved him, although on that score she understood. Women had a hard enough time figuring out the variations in hosiery sizes. Mick, though, had taken to the problem like a cancer scientist with a cure in all the data if he could just *see* it. "Look, I know I can get this if you just give me a few more minutes," he'd insisted.

"We're going home now, Dad," Noel had sang out.

"Now," Angie had echoed.

"Just hold on," Mick had said.

Kat had gently, firmly, repressively taken his arm.

Now she had the brief inclination to put her head in her arms. He'd tried so damned hard. He was determined to be a good father, even if it killed him. It nearly had. Killed the three of them.

And she was exhausted. She wasn't cut out to play diplomat/referee between a father and his daughters;

she was even less suited to play the feminine authority just because she was female.

Mick wasn't a threat. All afternoon he'd proven that. How could a man who made her laugh that hard, or exasperated her that much, be a threat to her sanity? He was just real. Human. Trying hard to make it through each day just as she was. Odd, how such a little detail like that could turn her heart to mush.

He lurched to a sitting position. The smell of earth and sea breezes clung to his skin; his shaggy tumble of hair looked as white as the moonlight. When she saw that his eyes looked serious, it did something to her heart, too. "Okay. Tell me straight—did I screw something up by going along?"

She considered telling him the truth—the "truth" that his daughters were hoping she'd tactfully pass on—but then she looked into his eyes again. What exactly did she owe those two little turkeys who'd preyed on her sympathy for weeks? "You did fine," she told him.

"Fine enough that I've earned a reward?"

"What kind of reward?" she asked suspiciously.

"The girls have been telling me for months that you have a horse in your living room. I figured they've been pulling my leg, but I admit they aroused my curiosity."

Mick knew she hadn't wanted to be in his kitchen that first night, she hadn't wanted him in her office, she certainly hadn't wanted him shopping today, and now she wasn't too hot on the idea of being alone in her house with him. But Mick had to wile his way into her living room. Wiling, sneaking and subterfuge went against every grain. Mick had always believed that honesty and respect were the keys to building a relationship—any relationship.

Unfortunately those concepts weren't worth beans with Kat.

"Would you like a very quick lemonade or iced tea?" she asked him.

"Either one would be fine." He hadn't missed that "very quick." If Kat had her way, he wasn't going to be here long.

For the brief moment she was out of sight in the kitchen, he explored, more curious than he wanted to be, less satisfied than he'd hoped.

In a hundred ways, the living room was distinctively Kat's. She'd chosen a color scheme of dramatic dark blue with touches of peach. The walls, couch, chair and rug were all the same elegant navy. Even the lamp in the corner had a base of dark blue glass, but there were delicate splashes of peach—silk flowers, pillows, a museum print over her mantel. All the furniture was antique, expensive, and dauntingly, maybe even defiantly, feminine—except for the carousel figure.

The wooden unicorn was garish and huge. Its mane was gold, its saddle scarlet and emerald. Her living room was too small for extras, and the unicorn was life-size. Only a woman with an uncontrollable romantic streak would have considered it a prize. Mick figured the unicorn was a helpful clue to understanding Kat. Very helpful. It was like being handed a red puzzle piece in an all-blue puzzle.

Why would a warm, empathetic, vibrantly attractive and whimsically romantic woman sleep alone?

"He fits in just like a Democrat at the Republican national convention, doesn't he?"

Mick turned to see Kat coming in with a tray, which held two glasses of iced tea and a small plateful of crackers and dips. When she set it on the coffee table, her white shorts rode high on her thighs and her hair skimmed her back, the color of silk on fire. His throat was suddenly dry. "You didn't have to go to all that trouble."

"Nonsense, it won't take you ten minutes to finish it. I know your daughters; they had to inherit their appetites from somewhere, and the best I can do is hors d'oeuvre a guest to death because I don't really cook." She motioned to her unicorn. "I found him at an estate sale, although he wasn't on the auction list. He was headed for a brush pile, until I took one look and fell in love." Suddenly all polite Southern hospitality, she handed him a cracker generously heaped with dip.

Mick only needed one bite to figure out how she intended to shorten his visit. If Kat expected him to dive for the iced tea, though, she was doomed to disappointment. He could handle hot peppers. Whether he could handle Kat was a different problem entirely. "Delicious," he murmured.

"Just wait until you try the others," she said genially.

Regrettably, she was too old to spank. "Do you have family around here?"

She shook her head. "My parents and grandmother live in Louisiana. Shreveport. And I have an older brother, Damon, who migrated to Atlanta about ten years ago. He shows up periodically, usually with his dirty laundry and never with any warning. I regularly threaten to strangle him."

Possibly, but he heard the warmth and love in her voice. "You sound close." He tried her couch, and discovered it was made for women with no back support, and no place for a man's knees. He'd already guessed that she hadn't decorated with the anticipation of any man being around.

"We are close, luckily. Not that I'm prejudiced, but my family's extraordinarily special. Have another one, Mick." All sass and sparkle, she handed him another cracker—with a different dip. The dare in her eyes was as mischievous—or as vulnerable—as a warning.

He took the cracker, primarily to let her know that if she could dish out horseradish, he could take it. This time, though, he had the sense to have the glass of iced tea handy. He needed it. The second dip cleared his sinuses.

Once he stopped breathing steam, he settled back. "So, you have a family you're close to, but no one in Charleston. Yet five years ago, you picked up sticks and moved here lock, stock, and barrel?"

"Your girls," she said firmly, "are probably still up and wondering where you are."

"They know where I am. They sent me here, to see your carousel horse, and so that you'd have a chance to deliver a lecture about how fathers shouldn't embarrass their children by shopping with them." He smiled when that very small, very delectable jaw of hers dropped a quarter of an inch. She even forgot herself and sank on the edge of the couch next to him. "Try one." He motioned to one of her lethal dips. "What was the guy's name in Shreveport?"

"Heavens, did I miss something in this conversation?"

"You haven't missed anything yet, Red, but I'll let you know if you do. And I'm leaving soon, but not yet. So you might as well kick off your sandals and at least try and relax."

"And here I was waiting for your permission."

"Lord, you're sassy. How can you take it so lightly?"

"Take what so lightly?"

He shook his head, and his voice lowered to the rasp of suede. "You were so exasperated with me in that earring store that you could hardly talk, then my hand brushed your shoulder and you forgot how mad you were. You couldn't stop laughing when I was handling those Easter-egg containers of panty hose, until you were trying to hustle me out of the store. The minute you grabbed my arm, your cheeks flushed and you started walking like you'd swallowed a cupful of starch."

"I was thinking about your girls!"

"So was I. Trying the whole afternoon to do the right thing for Noel and Angie. Only anytime I'm near you, I feel like I've been hit with a double whiskey on an empty stomach. And you—" he plucked a strand of her hair and tucked it neatly behind her ear "—kiss back with a dangerous responsiveness. All these years living next door to you, Kat, and I doubt either of us knew the attraction was there. You're worried about it?"

"I..." She heard her voice, more a whisper than sound. Nick's fingers had only sifted through her hair for seconds, yet his warmth lingered and his intense blue eyes rested gently on her face. It would be smarter to fib, to deny she felt any attraction, to tactfully suggest he'd misinterpreted her "responsiveness."

Only she couldn't lie. Not with him. "Yes, I'm worried," she said softly.

"And so am I. In fact, you couldn't possibly be more wary of starting something than I am, Red." She had a cracker crumb on the corner of her bottom lip. He used his thumb to brush it off, and watched her eyes dilate. "Since we both feel the same way, there's no reason we can't both be totally honest. It's been too long for me, and I'm in no hurry to take on something I'm not sure of. You feel about the same?"

"I . . . yes." She was terrified he was going to find another crumb.

"I wouldn't know how to woo a woman with roses and moonlight." The collar of her shirt revealed a great deal of her long white throat. He focused where her pulse was beating like a freight train. "And I keep having the feeling that you're not looking for roses and moonlight. At least right now. Is that right?"

"That's absolutely true, Mick, and—"

"The chemistry's special, but any chemistry is disturbing if both people don't feel comfortable with it. But we can both make the honest choice to ignore it, can't we?"

His hand had drifted to her shoulder. Actually not his whole hand. His arm was resting on the back of the couch and just his fingers drifted down, making the lightest fringe-tickle of contact with her shoulder. Lord, the room was warm.

"Kat?"

"We just completely ignore it," she agreed vibrantly. "Good grief, we're grown adults. What's chemistry, anyway?"

"Exactly, and we also live next door. You're important to my daughters. I don't want to do anything to mess that up, which is exactly why I brought all this up. The last thing I want you to feel is awkward or nervous around me, and I thought if we talked frankly—''

Kat nodded in complete understanding. Sort of. The whole conversation should have been a source of enormous relief. Given the choice, she'd have avoided a discussion of attraction like the plague—but that was her problem. It obviously wasn't Mick's, and in his forthright manner he'd both taken the subject out of the closet and put it to bed. He wasn't going to push it. *He's over June more than he realizes,* she thought, but that wasn't the point. Mick wanted a friend for his daughters and maybe a woman around whom he could talk to comfortably and honestly.

She was safe. Any real threat that he wanted intimacy between them had never even existed.

He smiled and stood up. She stood up, too, but her knees suddenly felt as steady as rotten timbers. *Boy, do you feel safe, Kat.*

With a wink and a grin, he held out his hand. "Friends?"

Friends, her foot. Friends, her behind. In the past two weeks every time Mick had mentioned the word "friends," she'd ended up in trouble. If he said that seven-letter word even one more time, Kat was going to bop him right in the old sheboggan. She was going to bring him to his knees. She was going to level him. She was going to...

"There's nothing else to bring in, Kat. Noel's already down at the beach. I'm going to head there, too."

"Fine, honey," Kat said gaily.

"You sure you don't need me for anything else?"

"Heavens, no."

Once Angie was gone, Kat plucked ten loaves of bread from the grocery sacks and shot them onto the counter like bullets. Heaven knew why Mick had bought ten loaves of bread . . . but then, heaven knew what she was doing in his cabin on Hunting Island.

She couldn't see the ocean from the kitchen window, but it was so close she could hear the waves and taste the lick of a tangy salt breeze. Mick's cottage was nestled behind a dune in a woods of palmetto and huge slash pine. Kat had assumed there would be people around because he'd told her the property nearly bordered a huge state park. So far all she'd seen were the lush tropical woods and about five million birds.

Inside, sun poured in through a window and onto the rough log walls and pine-planked floor. The cabin only had four rooms. Two were bedrooms, each lined with double sets of bunk beds. The kitchen opened onto the main living area. The furniture wasn't fancy, just big. The man-size couch was cushioned so thick a woman could fall in and never find her way out, the stone fireplace was big enough to roast an elephant and the storage closet was loaded with sports and fishing gear.

Kat rubbed two hot, damp fingers on her temples. June had so obviously belonged here. She so obviously didn't. Her forte was lace and garnets and the Victorian tea hour.

Taking steaks out of another grocery bag, she mentally damned Mick for fast-talking her into this weekend. He'd given her some confusing speech about his needing help with the girls.

She'd fallen for that line before. Ten days ago, he'd lured her to a picnic at dusk. Another hot afternoon, he'd coaxed her into a riverboat tour of the Charleston Harbor with him and the girls. A few nights ago, he'd shown up at her back door with a bottle of wine, claiming he was desperate for a place to hide out because Noel had bought a new rock tape.

Every time he'd appealed to her as a friend. Every time she'd been suckered in. And every time that unprincipled man had tucked an embrace into the encounter. Nothing too heavy, nothing too hot. It always began with a little touch, a little squeeze, a kiss that started as friendly, and then exploded. Mick always stopped. Just not until she was shaky from the inside out.

If a woman pulled that nonsense, she'd be labeled a tease.

Kat clapped a quart of milk onto the counter. Mick was worse than a tease. Damn him, he was making her a part of his life, a part of his family. And double damn him, Kat knew she couldn't be, but she also knew precisely why she'd let herself be conned into this weekend.

That horrible, wretched, sinfully disgusting man was opening up in front of her eyes. Talking with his daughters like he hadn't talked to his daughters in years. Taking the time to have fun instead of working twenty-four hours a day. And laughing—how could she not want to hear him laugh after all his years of grieving?

Kat heaved the potatoes out of the last sack. She'd helped him. She knew she had. There was no crime in caring for Mick. The crime was in the deception she was playing on herself.

Every time he pulled her into his arms, she conveniently forgot her "little problem." Well? She'd loved her ex-fiancé, but she'd never laughed with him like she did with Mick. She'd wanted Todd, but never with this razor-sharp urgency, this wild, winsome surge of yearning. If Mick took her to bed, couldn't it be different? Wasn't there a chance?

Her heart whispered *try*. Her head delivered a flat *don't be stupid, Kathryn*. If she'd only known one man, she'd known Todd well. They'd not only loved each other, but he'd been kind, considerate, understanding, careful. They hadn't tried once; they'd tried a dozen times. And every scene of intimacy had ended in the humiliation and embarrassment of pain.

"Everything okay?"

"Just fine, Mick," she sang out.

She fed a dozen more pop cans into the refrigerator, straightened up and peered into the last grocery sack. Nothing else to unpack; it was empty. Like her head.

A damp strand of hair tickled her cheek. She pushed at it. She had to get smart. She had to get tough. Helping Mick was one thing, but encouraging a real relationship—an intimate relationship—was another. *It's very easy, Kathryn. The next time he tries to kiss you, think stone. Think icebergs. Think rock.*

"Hey, slowpoke. When are you going to get those clothes off?"

Now there was a loaded question. She swiveled on her heel to face the beach bum in the doorway. The derelict had sandy feet, frayed swimming trunks, far too much bare, bronzed skin and a pretzel in his mouth. She tried to think rock, but her pulse was already racing.

Having some sanity left, though, she propped her hands on her hips and looked the big tease up and down with a schoolmarm's frown. "What happened to the chronic workaholic I used to know from Charleston?"

He fed her half his pretzel and steered her toward the "girls" bedroom. "The same thing that's going to happen to you—exposure to a little sun, a little breeze and a little ocean. As soon as you strip off all those extra clothes."

All those extra clothes consisted of a small green tank top and shorts. From the look in his eyes, she should have chosen to wear her most repressive whalebone corset. But good grief; it was 105 degrees in the shade. She made a point of saying: "Don't get your hopes up, Larson. I tend toward conservative bathing suits."

"What, no string bikini?"

"Nope."

"No suit cut so high you get a sunburn in awkward places?"

"Redheads have to worry about sunburn in all places, and it's okay, you don't have to come in. I've been putting on my own bathing suit for several years now."

"You can," he said in amazement four minutes later, and darn it, he made her laugh. Maybe it wasn't so different than shorts, but she'd dreaded his seeing her in a bathing suit. Bathing suits could be taken as an advertisement for what a woman had to physically offer, and Kat, always honest, had taken care not to advertise for years. No matter how demure her white maillot, though, she felt...displayed. She was just too aware that the promise of bare skin was a promise she couldn't keep.

Mick could have been nice. He could have been sweet and sensitive and perceptively ignored her flushed cheeks. Not him.

"I'll be damned!" He circled her faster than a rabid dog, patted her fanny, plucked at her shoulder strap and then wolf whistled. Maybe his eyes had a hint of dangerous blue, but his clowning teenage-boy act still had her laughing.

"I'll be damned," he repeated. "A female who actually wears a suit she can swim in. I thought the only reason a woman went to the beach was to slather on sun lotion and paint her toenails." He glanced at her toes, and touched his hand to her heart. "Good Lord, no paint. What will Noel say?"

"As soon as I find my backup—your daughters," Kat said. "You're going to be sorry you were ever born."

"Oh, yeah?"

"You think you're so big, Larson? You won't weigh patootties under water. If I were you, I'd start praying."

"I am, I am." Before she could blink, he was loading her arms with terry cloth. "You carry the towels. A man can't be expected to pray and carry towels, too."

She chased him out the door, almost as if...she were having a good time. Almost as if it felt as natural to play with Mick as it did to talk to him, and be with him, and to feel this crazy wild surge of laughter and love filling her up every time she was near him.

If she didn't know better, she might even believe she was falling in love with him.

Luckily she knew better than to let that happen.

Five

Most of Hunting Island was made up of state park-
land, and in the heat of the summer its shoreline was
packed. Few, though, wandered as far as Mick's jag-
ged strip of white beach. There wasn't a soul in sight,
which suited him just fine.

Sea oats and swamp grasses swayed on the dunes.
This late in the afternoon the tide was sneaking in, one
bubbling wave at a time. Gulls soared over the shallows, checking out dinner but too lazy to work for it
yet. The sky was still a blinding white, but the sun had
lost its baking heat. Mick raised himself on an elbow
to lift his shirt from Kat's shoulders. Earlier, her
fragile skin would have burned to a crisp if he hadn't
protected it.

She stirred from his touch but didn't really waken,
which gave him a few more minutes to look his fill.

The view would have aroused a saint. Until she woke up, he could look all he wanted.

One suit strap had slipped off her shoulder, and she was sprawled on her stomach with one leg tucked up. A ribbon of sand had dried on her nape. After their swim, her hair had been dripping in long wet ropes. Now it was fluffed up, a tangled swath of sun-kissed auburn.

He found a light spray of freckles dusting her collarbone, and another cache at the dip of her bathing suit. Her fanny, which he'd become an expert on in the past hour, was too slim, too small, and had to be the most erotic, enticing, sassy slope of rump he'd ever seen. He considered whether he'd developed a recent prejudice.

He decided, humorously, that he had, but he wasn't going to worry about it. If a man was going to go crazy with worry, Kat provided ample possibilities without dwelling on the trivial.

She could outwork and outcompete any man he knew in business, yet fell for a hopelessly frivolous carousel unicorn. She talked common sense to his daughters, then tore through town daring red lights. She was hardheaded and stubborn and she faced trouble head-on. That first night, she'd tackled him about the girls because she simply didn't know how to walk away from something she thought was wrong. Strong? The lady was a brick.

She was also the most sensual woman he'd ever met, not only in looks and temperament but in touch. She drove him damn near crazy with her responsiveness, but she was scared off at the line of any real intimacy. And the operative word, Mick had finally concluded, was *scared*. Hurt scared, gut scared, blind scared.

He didn't understand why. He didn't understand *her*, and it had taken him several weeks to accept that he didn't have to. No other woman had ever made him feel this tug, this draw, this intimate sense of completeness. No other man was going to lie beside Kat—not in the sand, and not in a bed.

Those things he understood just fine.

She hadn't meant to fall asleep, he knew, and he was the one who deserved the nap. Between his daughters and Kat, he'd been dunked, raced and challenged to any water game where it was possible to pit three against one. Kat didn't like things fair. She liked the odds all on her side. She also liked a full quota of chaperons.

Beside him, she stretched sinuously, like a cat, and her lids opened sleepily. Momentarily she was disoriented, not realizing that his shadow covered her as possessively as his gaze. Momentarily her eyes met his and need, raw and honest, charged between them. Momentarily she told him what he needed to know, that she wanted him—that she cared. And the most potent draw of all: that she needed him.

Not surprising him in the least, she abruptly jerked awake, tore her eyes from his and began a frantic search of the beach. "Where are Noel and Angie?"

Poor baby. He hated to tell her that her chaperons had taken a powder. "There's a camp store in the state park, which is Angie's favorite hangout. Ride a bike up there, and she inevitably runs into a group of kids her own age from the campground. And Noel found some teenagers playing volleyball down the beach. She had her eye on one poor unsuspecting boy with freckles. I doubt we'll see either of them until they're starving."

"When did all that action happen?"

"While you were asleep."

"I wasn't asleep," Kat assured him. "I couldn't have been. I never nap during the day."

"While you weren't sleeping," he said mildly, "I covered you up so you wouldn't burn. Except for your nose." He patted the pink nose in question, almost making her smile, but she was clearly distracted.

"Mick?"

"Hmmm?" He couldn't wait any longer to brush away the bit of sand on her nape. While he was in the vicinity, he let his fingers thread through her hair. Sand was mixed in with the silky strands. Even so, Rumpelstiltskin had never spun gold like this.

"I believe you told me that the girls had 'outgrown' their love of camping. That they didn't want to come because there was nothing to do here. And the reason I had to come with you this weekend was to help entertain them."

"Did I tell you that?"

"You did."

"Ah, well. I lied." Judiciously he adjusted her bathing suit strap. She didn't seem to realize that she was raised on her elbow, exposing him to a view of one small, shadowed breast. Fixing her strap gave him a chance to look like a gentleman.

"Mick?" Possibly she wasn't fooled. She lifted his hand like a mother who was removing a cookie from a toddler. There was so much patience in her expression that he had to grin.

"Hmmm?"

"I will discuss your lying habits with you shortly. For the present, however, there seems to be a bird about six inches from my face."

"Didn't you wonder why we bought ten loaves of bread for one short weekend? Sit up, very slowly, very quietly. He'll eat right out of your hand if you want him to, but be prepared."

"Prepared for what?"

The minute he reached behind him and handed her a loaf of bread, the first grape-winged gull was joined by a friend. Kat hadn't untwisted the wrapper before a dozen gulls squawked up in the air. North, south, east, west, the message traveled that they had a sucker on the hook, and the flocks soared in.

Kat started chuckling and couldn't stop. "For heaven's sake, help me!"

"You're doing fine." He watched her shredding bits of bread at the speed of sound. The sunlight streamed through her hair, caught on her laughter. She rocked on her heels, a sea nymph surrounded by a hundred strutting, fluttering conventioneers.

"The whole loaf's going to be gone in two seconds—stop that, you thief!" One bold gull went straight for the bread wrapper. Another pushed his sister out of the way, and a third hovered in midair, expecting to catch his treat in flight. "I thought the critters on this island were supposed to be wild."

"You call this manners?"

"I call it wonderful." Her eyes softened to a dark, liquid brown when a bird plucked a tidbit right out of her hand.

"Don't fall too hard for the greedy scavengers. We're talking a love 'em and leave 'em mentality. Once the bread's gone, they won't remember your name."

"That's disgustingly cynical, Mick."

"But dead true."

"I don't care. Aren't they beautiful?"

He thought *she* was beautiful. The nap had refreshed her; he knew damn well she worked too hard. He also knew that she was smart. Smart enough to have found an excuse for the weekend if she didn't want to be here, smart enough to avoid his kisses if she didn't want them. And smart enough to know that he wasn't a man who played, not with a woman's emotions or his own.

They were spiraling, dangerously fast, toward intimacy. She had to know it. She may not know that when they were together, he felt as if he'd never been alive before. Not as a man. He touched Kat and it was all there. What was possible, what he'd missed, everything that could and should be between a man and a woman.

Some guy had burned her. Hell, it didn't take a degree in psychology to figure that out. The pain from that burn kicked in every time he crossed a certain sexual line, and Mick would have worried more about that if not for the obvious. He knew who he was as a lover; he knew what would happen when they made love.

Kat had reason to be nervous, all right, but only because he intended to immerse that wary redhead in more satisfaction than she could handle.

Soon. At the moment he was content to watch the sun, wind and sea work its magic on Kat. The island had always been a source of renewal for him. Its spell was sneaking up on her. He shook his head, watching her cavort down the beach, madly throwing bread crumbs and giggling in the sun. Had he once been positive she wouldn't enjoy the simple pleasures?

Even when the bread was long gone, she didn't want to leave the gulls. He had to swing an arm around her shoulder and murmur sexy sweet nothings about steak, baked potatoes, burned marshmallows. "But we can't start dinner without the girls, Mick."

"Trust me. They'll be here." Back at the cabin, he built a teepee of twigs in the fire pit while she showered. When she came back out, she was wearing a French braid and a short yellow jumpsuit that zipped to her throat. He tampered with the zipper until there was a shadow of cleavage to tease him—she let that happen. When he came out of the shower wearing only cutoffs, she obviously still had her mind on zippers because she leveled a stare at his, making him laugh.

"It's buried pretty deep, Red, but I think you just may have an itsy bitsy bawdy streak buried deep in your closet," he drawled.

She flushed to the roots of her hair. "I don't. You obviously misunderstood."

"No, I didn't. For almost a whole afternoon, you forgot to be careful." His voice softened for her. "I like you natural and easy with me. Don't fight it."

It was obviously the wrong thing to say. She tensed up, emotionally retreated as if she'd done something criminally wrong in flirting with him. They still talked, but every few moments her head swiveled toward the woods. "Are you sure I shouldn't try to find the girls?"

"They'll be here," he repeated. The sky turned from white to a deep sea blue as the sun plummeted in the west. By then, foiled potatoes were baking in the coals. He fiddled with the grill and started forking on the marinated steaks.

Two minutes to formal dining time, Kat's chaperons showed up—with reinforcements. A freckle-faced boy was trying to hide behind Noel. Angie had a scrawny sidekick with a wholesome grin.

Kat immediately relaxed. "So that's why you put on so many steaks," she murmured.

"We may not have done this in a long time, but old patterns are hard to break. My daughters are not shy."

Neither was Kat . . . with his daughters. The extra company took off after dinner, but his three lingered by the fire. By then, the sun had long set on a whistling-still night, and the coals, spitting hot, glittered orange and yellow in the darkness. Kat squeezed in on a log between Noel and Angie, with a long stick in her hand, and burned her tongue on more scorched marshmallows than either of the other two.

Not surprisingly Mick was suckered into the hot seat between knees—Kat's and Angie's—and given the job of marshmallow distribution. Payment was their most pitifully burned offerings. Contentment seeped through him. Because of his workaholic obsession for the past two years, he could have lost this with his girls—their ability to enjoy each other, to just be together as a family. He'd recognized his mistakes before meeting Kat, but it was her hands-on-hips-furious lecture that first night that had spurred him to action.

Whether she knew it or not, she had an equally powerful effect on his girls. He listened, disarmed to hear the three of them talk nonstop. June had mothered his daughters. Kat questioned, argued and challenged them. She had the authority of an age difference, but she also respected them as equal and interesting human beings. He didn't know that Noel had opinions about the homeless, that Angie had been reading about the environment. He also didn't know a whole lot about differences in makeup, but he got an earful.

In due time they ran out of marshmallows, and yawns slowed down the conversation. It was past ten. Mick started banking the fire.

"Noel and I are going to take our sleeping bags to the beach, okay?" Angie bounded over to throw her arms around his neck. Only from his youngest would he have taken that marshmallow-sticky smack on his cheek. "Thanks, Dad."

"Wait a minute. I don't remember saying yes."

"That's okay, you know you're going to let us. We already know all the rules: no swimming, set up high behind the tide line and scat if anybody else shows up on the beach." Angie grinned, the little devil had known for years he was putty for that grin, and then raced for the cabin and the sleeping bags.

Noel's good-night hug was just as exuberant, but then she pointed a finger at him like a schoolmarm. "Don't worry about Angie, you know I'll watch out for her. You two just behave yourselves, take care of Kat and don't stay up too late."

When the two had hiked out of sight, he scratched a tickle at the back of his neck and gave Kat a rueful look. "Give it to me straight. Have I lost total control?"

Kat chuckled, but she was instantly aware that they were alone. In the dark. And that her bunking companions had just deserted ship. "I think you're paying the price for raising them to be independent."

"Too independent?"

Her gaze darted away from the too dark, too empty cabin, instantly diverted by the uncertain quality in Mick's voice. The only time she had ever heard Mick less than sure was on the subject of his daughters. "You said it yourself, Mick. How can you possibly raise a child to be too independent?" she asked gently. "How can anyone develop character if they haven't had the freedom to try things, to make mistakes, to test out who they are and what they can do?"

"Yeah, that's the principle." Blocking her view of the cabin, Mick reached down to claim her hand. He pulled her up and close, but only for a moment. "The reality's a little different. Every time I see a boy around Noel, I have this instant urge to check out convent tuition costs."

"She's testing her feminine mettle," Kat agreed wryly. "But at least she's busy trying to charm the entire male population. It's when she singles out one boy that you'll undoubtedly need tranquilizers."

"Did you?"

"Did I what?" They seemed to be walking deep under the swaying tropical palmettos. The night was magical. Fireflies danced in the moonlight-speckled path and it was happening to Kat again. She was supposed to be careful and wary around Mick. She was supposed to remember that she wasn't like other women and that she had no business encouraging a relationship with him.

She was supposed to not feel a heart-singing zing when he loped an arm around her shoulder and teasingly repeated the question he obviously thought she was avoiding. "Did you test your feminine mettle at Noel's age?"

"To the limit. Past the limit," she admitted humorously. Maybe it was the cool sand under her toes, the whisper of a summer breeze, the scent of sea and trees. But the personal doors she found so hard to open with people just wouldn't stay closed, not with him. "I dated the wildest boys in school and broke every curfew my parents set. My poor mother! I know darn well she started going gray when I was in high school, and all for nothing."

He dropped his arm and amused her with his leonine scowl. "Doesn't sound like nothing to me."

She laughed, and spilled out a little more. "I was all show and no go. Never missed a Saturday night at the local lovers' lane, but the most active thing I ever did was direct traffic. Hells bells, I stuffed my bras with tissue all through high school. Do you think I'd have let a boy discover that?"

There was a moment's silence, but his eyes glinted at her in the darkness. "You didn't really do that."

"Direct traffic?"

"Stuff your bra."

"Sure, I did. And you can quit choking on that chuckle, Larson. I didn't do anything that wasn't a time-honored ritual. Puritans used to sew in tucks; Victorian teenagers used to stuff their whalebone with batting and I don't see that the girls in this generation have changed so much. Haven't you noticed that Noel is slightly...lopsided from day-to-day?"

"Are you trying to tell me that my daughter—?"

"Isn't and couldn't naturally be that lumpy." She won a throaty chuckle from him, but was more conscious of his palm sliding down her spine. He was steering her toward the left fork in the path, out of the woods and toward the beach. Once over the dune, sand mounded beneath the arch of her feet and the ocean was suddenly there, big and black and endless.

She loved the ocean, but not at night, not alone. Mick took the space between her and that dark abyss.

Kat thought fleetingly that Mick would always do that with the woman he cared for—come between her and all those dark abysses in life.

She mentally pulled herself up short when she realized where the direction of that thought and emotion was taking her. "I told you what I was like as a teenager to be honest with you, Mick. I really am probably the last person to give you responsible, respectable advice about your daughters." She added swiftly, "They have to miss June."

Mick heard her but didn't respond. Kat might want to talk about June, but he didn't. She'd given him another puzzle piece that, like her carousel horse, didn't fit. He could far too zealously picture a redhead who'd teased half the boys in the county in the local lovers' lane...but it wouldn't reconcile with a grown woman who'd chosen celibacy for the past five years.

"Mick?"

She was obviously going to worry the subject until he dealt with it. He sighed. Maybe it was time. "I know the girls miss June." He sucked in a lungful of sea air. "On a rare night, I try to convince myself that I'm doing all right as a father. But that's not to say I ever have illusions I could take their mother's place. It's tough on them both."

"And just as tough on you. I'm sure you miss her. June never made any secret about how happy she was." Kat's smile was gentle. "She must have told me a hundred times how you were the only man on earth she could have lived with."

She'd said the last comment to make him smile, yet the moonlight caught his austere profile, the glint of some unexpected emotion in his eyes. Pain? He said,

"I hope and believe she was happy with what we had together."

"You can't doubt that? She never made any secret about it. You two were perfect. The whole neighborhood knew." Kat groped through suddenly troubled waters. She hadn't started the subject to probe, but because Mick talked easily about his daughters. She'd just wanted him to know she was there for him if he wanted to discuss June as well. "Weren't you? Happy?" she whispered.

Mick's voice was flat, quiet, blunt. "We were married. And if she hadn't died, we would still be married."

"Which tells me how you feel about loyalty and fidelity and marriage vows, but that wasn't what I asked you. I asked you if you were happy."

"She was. And I have to believe that, or else fourteen years of my life didn't make much sense. Come here, Red." When she didn't immediately move, he reached out and cupped her nape with his big palm. He hauled her against him until their hips bumped as they walked. "Getting pretty brazen these days, asking me personal questions, acting like you have a right to know."

"I don't have any right to know—"

"Yeah, you do. If you want to know if I've forgotten June, the answer is no. I haven't, won't, and don't expect to forget someone who was a part of my life for that many years."

"Of course not."

"But what you really want to know, what you were pretty sure you were going to hear I think, was that I have yet to get over the loss of my wife. I have good memories of June, Red, but nothing that could ever threaten you. I don't see her when I look at you. I don't want her when I touch you. I'm not lonely for what I had. When I'm with you, I'm damned lonely for what could be." His eyes roamed over her face, slow, real slow, and her heart suddenly kicked in like a rocket booster.

"I—" Kat told herself that Mick had completely misunderstood why she'd brought up his wife. Completely. Only his gaze held hers like a magnet. Damn, but his eyes were blue, even in the darkness, and she was afraid he understood too much. Like how deeply and thoroughly a woman could lie to herself, for example.

"You were starting to say something?"

"I forgot whatever it was," she admitted.

"Good, because that's enough of serious subjects. The night's warm and the stars are out, and five bucks says I can beat you to that piece of driftwood high up on the beach. I'll give you a head start to the count of five."

"Mick—"

"One—you still dawdling, Red? I could have sworn you wouldn't turn down a dare. Two..."

He drawled the word "two," staring down at her from his towering height. Maybe he was in the mood for some crazy, silly race, but Kat was feeling stunned. It had never occurred to her that Mick had been privately, painfully unhappy with June. More than that, Kat understood that she'd run into a door that was permanently closed in Mick. The sign on that door was honor. Mick was not a man who would ever say a negative word about his wife, not in this life.

"Three..."

She never made a conscious decision, but simply acted on instinct. The subject was not one he could talk about and he wanted it dropped. He wanted to play. He needed to play, and Kat's response was automatic.

She ran, kicking sand in her wake.

His blond head streaked by her, then slowed down like the hare in the fable, arrogantly sure of his male-dominant win. She caught his grin and suddenly matched it. Adrenaline started pumping and her legs started aching, and running, just running as wild as hell, felt wonderful.

The surf roared next to them and the stars showered light, and she was panting and laughing as freely as Mick when she reached his fallen driftwood. Being no gentleman he'd beat her there, and he wanted his money.

"Forget that, you turkey. I never shook hands on that bet."

He was huffing as hard as she was but his eyes narrowed dangerously. "Don't tell me you're a welsher."

"I'm not a welsher. I never bet!"

"You ran. You lost. You owe."

"Only a man who won would reason that way."

"So you admit I won!" He slugged his fists on his hips. "You have two pockets in that jumpsuit thing you're wearing. I'll bet you have a little cash tucked in one of them. Like maybe my five."

"I don't. Good grief, you keep this up, I'm going to smell your breath. No, Larson." She backed away from the driftwood, edging closer toward the ocean. He stalked. She retreated. He was grinning, and her heart was suddenly beating, beating, beating. "I'm telling you, I *promise* you, I don't have any money in my pockets.''

''You don't seriously think I'd trust the word of a welsher?''

''Behave yourself.'' The Atlantic at her back was hardly a help. She put a hand in front of her as if she thought it would stop a charging bull.

''I just want to see what's in your pockets.''

''Don't you touch me, Mick Larson. You come any closer and you're going to be sorry. You're going to be eating sand. You're going to be—''

She'd turned halfway to run when he pounced, his right hand snaking around her waist and his left hand diving into her pocket. She felt his fingers through terrycloth at the intimate crease in her thigh. She was still choking back laughter when her pulse rate suddenly soared off the chart.

''Damn. Nothing in this one,'' he said innocently, and spun her around to face him.

''You reprobate. You overgrown adolescent. You—''

His kiss cut off her threats. Either that or she forgot them. Her arms seemed to be dangling in midair, her lungs stranded without a breath of air.

It wasn't like being swept away. It wasn't like the rest of the world blurred when he touched her. The crash of surf roared in her ears. She felt the waves sip at her feet, could feel the sting of sticky salt on her flesh. The whole night was flavored with heat. And Mick. She could hear his soughed breath, feel his leather-rough palms sliding up her bare arms. She could taste Coke and marshmallows on his tongue. She could taste him.

Every time she felt his arms around her, she knew she shouldn't, couldn't, risk this. She had no excuse for coming with him this weekend; she had no excuse for inviting a relationship. She knew what Mick wanted—it had nothing to do with "friends" or helping his daughters—and by responding with honest emotion, she had given him every reason to believe she wanted the same thing.

And there was the rub, because she did want exactly what he did. Nothing had ever felt as good as his big warm hands gliding over her skin. She wanted his tongue; she wanted his hips pushed hard and erotically against her, and she wanted the feel of his rough, coarse hair rippling around her fingers.

Unlike the child who'd been burned once, she just didn't learn. She kept coming back for more. She kept coming back for Mick, because it was so powerfully, wonderfully special with him. It wasn't just hard. It was becoming impossible for her to believe that anything could go wrong if the man was Mick.

Mick had fully intended to steal a few kisses. He'd intended to steal more than a few. He already knew the exact point where Kat would be scared off, and he knew exactly what she did to him when she responded wildly. There was a fragile, explosive line where teasing stopped being fun, where desire could become a tortuous, physical need. A man, a lover, who knew what he was doing could ride that line. He wasn't going to push her. He wanted Kat willing, not wary. Free, not unsure. And there was no question in Mick's mind that he had the control to pull back whenever he had to.

Only he hadn't planned on Kat. Always, her kisses had been winsome and sweet and responsive—even wild. But not desperate. Always, she'd let him know in subtle, physical ways when she wanted him to stop.

He shifted his hands to her narrow hips, rubbing her against him. Hard. Deliberately. Carnally.

Kat didn't pull back. She rubbed back.

They sank to their knees in the sand, neither severing an openmouthed kiss involving tongues, tastes, promises. Their first kisses were electric. These could have short-circuited a power plant. She sent him definite physical messages, none involving a "no."

She was scared, he felt it, yet the fragility and femininity in Kat had all the flavor of hunger and a woman coming alive. Her fingers climbed his arms, slid over his shoulders and coiled in the sparse white hair on his chest. Her lips clung to his.

Mick tried to keep control, only he'd wanted, craved, dreamed Kat would touch him like this. Freely. Honestly. Not just with sexual need, but with need. The emotional soul-deep need of a woman who wanted him for completeness.

She would cut it off now, he was sure.

Only she didn't. Her small white hands slid down to the waistband of his cutoffs. Her mouth latched onto his, an aching kiss, a yearning kiss.

He rubbed a thigh between hers, announcing he was aroused and hot in a way she couldn't possibly misunderstand. Over the roar of surf, the whispered rustle of trees, she had to hear the whisper of a zipper sneaking down. He flipped the bra latch. Her breasts were white in the moonlight. Tiny. Taut. Perfect. His tongue worked the nipples into little stones. She arched for those soft, slow, wet licks.

"Call it off, love." He knew his voice sounded rough, even harsh. "Honey, do it now. Because if you don't do it now—"

She slicked her hands through his hair and reached for a kiss.

"Dammit, Red—"

He kissed her mouth. He kissed her throat. He unzipped her jumpsuit the rest of the way, telling himself that it might have gotten beyond Kat, but he was stronger than that. There was no way he was going to make love to her for the first time on a public beach with sand digging in uncomfortable places and the ocean screaming in the background.

Carefully, shyly, tentatively, her fingers slid down to the bulging hardness in his jeans.

He suddenly didn't give a hoot in hell where they made love.

"Please, Mick . . ."

Her whisper was a call of need, sweet, low, desperate. He still had control, he promised himself.

"Please . . ."

He lost it. He totally and completely lost it. She was silky bare before he ended the next kiss. Lord! Her skin against the sand, her eyes against the moonlight and the warmth of her. . . .

He shucked his cutoffs. The way she looked at him, he'd have shucked his soul if she'd asked him. Willing was just a word. Kat needed him.

He framed her thighs around him. His weight and hardness caressed her softness. She could have been scared off then. She could have changed her mind. Her lashes lifted, her arms swept around his neck and she whispered, "Hurry. Now, Mick. Nothing's ever felt this right, not like this. With you. Please."

He had to take her. He had to, he wanted to, he was positive he would have died if he didn't. The surf roared in the distance, the sand gave for his weight on her weight. He tasted love, as he'd only dreamed of it. He tasted the allure of a woman wanting him, as only Kat had ever wanted him. He tasted need, denied him forever, and it tasted like her mouth, her skin, her fragrance. She was ready.

And at the first probe into her intimate nest, she cried.

He'd hoped, dreamed, anticipated that she would make a sound just like that.

Only her cry was supposed to be of pleasure.

Not pain.

Silhouette's

Best Ever "Get Acquainted" Offer

Look what we'd give to hear from you

6 FREE GIFTS 6

Return This Sticker
and Get 6 Gifts—FREE
Compliments of Silhouette

**GET ALL YOU ARE
ENTITLED TO—AFFIX STICKER
TO RETURN CARD—MAIL TODAY**

This is our most fabulous offer ever...
AND THERE'S STILL MORE INSIDE.
Let's get acquainted.
Let's become friends—

Look what we've got for you:

… A FREE 20k gold electroplate chain
… plus a sampler set of 4 terrific Silhouette Desire® novels, specially selected by our editors.

… PLUS a surprise mystery gift that will delight you.

All this just for trying our Reader Service!

If you wish to continue in the Reader Service, you'll get 6 new Silhouette Desire® novels every month—before they're available in stores. That's SNEAK PREVIEWS for just $2.24* per book— 26¢ less than the cover price—and FREE home delivery besides!

Plus There's More!

With your monthly book shipments, you'll also get our newsletter, packed with news of your favorite authors and upcoming books—FREE! And as a valued reader, we'll be sending you additional free gifts from time to time— as a token of our appreciation for being a home subscriber.

THERE IS NO CATCH. You're not required to buy a single book, ever. You may cancel Reader Service privileges anytime, if you want. All you have to do is write "cancel" on your statement or simply return your shipment of books to us at our cost. The free gifts are yours anyway. It's a super-sweet deal if ever there was one. Try us and see!

Get 4 FREE full-length Silhouette Desire® novels.

Plus

this lovely 20k gold
electroplate chain

Plus

a surprise
free gift

▼ PLUS LOTS MORE! MAIL THIS CARD TODAY ▼

Silhouette's Best-Ever "Get Acquainted" Offer

Yes, I'll try Silhouette books under the terms outlined on the opposite page. Send me 4 free Silhouette Desire® novels, a free electroplated gold chain and a free mystery gift.

225 CIS JAZA (U-S-D-03/90)

PLACE STICKER
FOR 6 FREE GIFTS
HERE

NAME _____

ADDRESS _____ APT. _____

CITY _____

STATE _____ ZIP CODE _____

Offer limited to one per household and not valid to current Silhouette Desire Subscribers. All orders subject to approval.
Terms and prices subject to change without notice.
© 1989 HARLEQUIN ENTERPRISES LTD.

PRINTED IN U.S.A.

Don't forget...

... Return this card today and receive 4 free books, free electroplated gold chain and free mystery gift.

... You will receive books before they're available in stores.

... No obligation to buy. You can cancel at any time by writing "cancel" on your statement or returning a shipment to us at our cost.

BUSINESS REPLY CARD

First Class   Permit No. 717   Buffalo, NY

Postage will be paid by addressee

Silhouette® Books
901 Fuhrmann Blvd.
P.O. Box 1867
Buffalo, NY 14240-9952

No Postage
Necessary
If Mailed
In The
United States

Six

Kat's eyes were closed, acting as a shutter to the tears that were backed up clear to her throat. It wasn't as if she was going to die. It wasn't as if she couldn't handle it. Pain was just . . . pain.

She wanted Mick inside her. Moments before she'd wanted him inside her like a clawing in her body, mind and soul. That hadn't changed. It was just . . . pain had a way of dousing even the most powerful sexual desire with a bucket of water. Every muscle in her body had locked and she burned like fire. There. At the precise spot where her sheath and his fullness created the most intimate bond a man and woman could have. Unfortunately it was a heck of a vulnerable spot to have to deal with pain.

And then she didn't have to deal with it. She heard Mick take one hard, shuddering breath. He withdrew. At least that part of his body withdrew. He rolled on his back with one arm coiled around her and clamped her cheek to his chest, not too gently. His heart was beating like a rocky, revved-up engine. She tried to lift her head. He hauled her closer.

"Maybe it'll be easier if we do this together. Breathe out, breathe in, real slow, real long breaths. Blank your mind of anything except the Red Sox's last loss. Hell, Red. If you think the Dodgers would work better, we'll try them." There was humor in his voice, but there was also grit, like he was doing his best to chew sand. His lips ironed her forehead, as hard as a stamped-on label. Again she tried to lift her head. Again, his arms clamped around her. "If you want to haul off and hit me, go ahead," he murmured gruffly.

"Hit you?"

"The sand, for God's sake. And out in the open. And coming at you like some rutting animal. I never lost my head like that when I was a teenager and my whole life was hormones. You do go to my head, Kat—not that that's any excuse for what I did." He heaved one last breath of control, and he almost managed gentleness when he cocked her chin. Blue, blue eyes pinned hers. "That's no excuse for what you did, either."

"Lord, I know . . . Mick, it was all my fault—"

"For not letting me know I was hurting you? You bet it was. Just when were you going to get around to mentioning you were in trouble?" Her lips moved, but they weren't producing any sound. They didn't have to. The look in her eyes said it all. "You weren't going to tell me, is that it? You were just going to let me go on?"

Guilt slammed at him. He shouldn't have raised his voice. Her lower lip started trembling and her face blanched. "I...didn't expect you to stop. I didn't think you could and I wouldn't have asked you to. Not...by then. And I thought I could handle it without your knowing."

Mick didn't need to hear anymore. His voice lowered to a murmur in the wind. "What the sam hill kind of lovers have you been to bed with, Red?" He threaded his fingers through her hair. At the tip of one strand was a tiny, tangled rubber band, all that was left of her French braid. "If you didn't know it before, know it now, a man can always stop. Sure, that can get a little touch and go on the timing." Later he would give himself enormous credit for that understatement. "But when one of us has a problem, we both have the problem. Got that? Anytime something isn't right, you say so. And so I know you've got that clear, say 'yes, Mick.'" The order was in his eyes.

"Yes, Mick."

But she wasn't off the hook yet. His gaze, worried, possessive, swept over her face. "I know I hurt you, so don't go all flustered and Victorian on me now. Are you okay? Could I have torn something? Are you still hurting?"

"I'm fine." She could feel the heat of color streaking up her cheeks. Unlike any other man she'd known, Mick naturally discussed feminine intimacies. She didn't. "I'm probably more fine than you are."

"Yeah?" He glanced down his moonlit body. "Don't worry about it. That'll cure real quick after a lap or two across the Atlantic. Besides, now we know for sure."

"For sure?"

"That you can't die from frustration," he said dryly. When she reached for her jumpsuit, he stole it away from her, stood up and then reached for her hands.

She didn't say anything when he pulled her underpants on backwards. She didn't say anything when he threaded her legs in the jumpsuit, pulled it up and started zipping. He didn't dress her like he would dress a child. Naked, the sea breeze rippling through his blond head, he dressed her with the total concentration of a lover. His palms lingered on her hips. He pulled the zipper up its track, but not before his kisses had made a preliminary run up the same track. He stuffed her bra in her pocket. He didn't like the bra. He liked the mounds of her breasts through terrycloth, and he brushed his thumbs over the tips through the material. When those tips hardened like buttons, he hardened like a rock.

He told her in a hundred ways that nothing had changed. He wanted her. She wanted him. One tiny setback hadn't turned him off, but magnified the feelings that were growing for her. He cared.

So much that she suddenly slid her arms around his waist and hung on. "Mick." Tears stung her eyes. "You weren't listening before but you have to listen now. It really wasn't your fault. At all. It was totally mine."

"I see. You're responsible for my showing the finesse of a Mack truck?"

"That's not the problem." She whispered hopelessly, "I'm frigid."

"Honey, it's tricky to hear you when you're talking to my chest."

She couldn't help that. On a subject this mortifying and painful, she couldn't face eye-to-eye contact.

"*Frigid*. At least I don't know what else to call it, but—"

She heard a rumbling in his chest like the beginnings of an earthquake. Startled, she lifted her head. He didn't even try to choke back a chuckle, and for the first time in an hour his eyes were crinkled with devilish humor. "Trust me. One thing you are not and could never be—not in this life, Red—is frigid."

He thought it was funny. Not a little funny. He thought it was real funny that she could even imagine herself frigid. Kat winged her MG down Calhoun, ran a yellow and let out the clutch.

Almost everyone who knew her thought she was a throwback to the Victorian era. She'd never asked a man out, never even called one except for business. She knew she was affectionate and warm with those she loved, but it was a heck of a jolt to her self-image to think Mick saw her as, well, hot. So hot that the idea of her being frigid struck Mick as belly-laughing funny.

She glanced at the rearview mirror. *He didn't get that impression out of a magician's hat, Kathryn Bryant. You've behaved completely different around Mick than you have with any other man.*

She knew that, which was why she had done an exceptional job of avoiding him for the past three days. Impatiently she shifted into third. The entire traffic in Charleston was driving slow this early August lunch hour. It had to be five million degrees and the humidity was worse. Anywhere skin touched skin, it stuck. Anything that could itch, itched.

Two pieces of paper fluttered on the leather seat next to her. One had been tacked to her back door, the other to her front door that morning. The notes held identical information—dinner tonight, five o'clock, wear boat shoes.

She could have ignored one note. Two was tougher. Larson was on to her. Like the coward that she was, she'd been hiding out for three days, not answering the phone, finding excuses to stay away from home and see to renovation projects away from the shop. Teenage girls acted with more maturity, Kat knew, but that hadn't stopped her from plotting all morning on how she could get out of this dinner.

You're real hot, all right, Bryant. Until it comes down to the crunch. Dammit, how could you have done that to him when you know how you are?

She swung into the alley behind the warehouse, killed the engine and grabbed her keys. Clouds hovered in the west, dark and promising. The heat wave hadn't broken in a month. The whole city was praying for rain, and the heaviness and gloom in the air had to be responsible for her mood. She was not just medium low, she felt on a level with a pit.

If it hadn't worked with Mick, it was never going to work. If you loved a man, if you had trust and empathy and respect heaped way up high on top of the passion and it still wasn't right, it was never going to be right.

She knew how she could get out of dinner tonight. She could simply sneak back home and retack his notes on the doors as if she'd never seen them. There were a hundred places she could hide out past five tonight, her office was an obvious choice. Heaven knew she had plenty of work.

Come on, Kat. You live next door to him. You're going to have to face him sometime.

She knew that. She just wanted that sometime to be later. A lot later. 1995, 1996. Not yet. No lectures on maturity or cowardice, okay, God? I'm being as honest as I know how. I can't handle this.

The bell jangled when she strode in. Georgia glanced up from the cash register. "Have a good lunch?"

"Fine. I'll guard the bank. You take a long one. It's too hot to do anything quick today."

"I had my lunch." Georgia lifted one of those dreadful protein diet drinks from under the counter, making Kat grimace. "And in the meantime, you had a phone call. Mick. He wanted to remind you that he was picking you up at five tonight."

Kat briefly considered picking up the priceless lace shawl on the counter and shredding it.

"And don't worry, Kathryn. He sounded concerned that you might get held up late here. I told him for sure you'd be free."

"Thanks so much." She couldn't wring Georgia's neck. She was too good a friend. Still, there was such a somnolent blandness in Georgia's expression that Kat was briefly tempted to offer her a rich, gooey cream puff. "Anything else happen? Tornado, phone call from the IRS? A robbery?"

"Nothing quite that disastrous—"

"Amazing," Kat murmured balefully.

"But you do happen to have a couple of visitors waiting for you in your office."

"Visitors?"

Mutt and Jeff were feasting on tall glasses of lemonade and raspberry tarts. The little blond with the crimped hair was swinging her legs from the corner of the desk, and the mousse-spiked brunette—dressed in red and white!—had taken over her office chair. "Don't you look terrific!" Kat complimented Noel and gave Angie a quick hug. "But what on earth brings you two downtown, and how'd you even get here?"

Both of them started talking at once.

"We pooled our money on a taxi," Angie admitted.

"We've wanted to see your store for forever, Kat, but even more than that we wanted to talk to you."

"We needed to talk to you," Angie corrected her sister. "This is important, and we couldn't talk anywhere where Dad could be around."

"Sounds serious," Kat said gently. It sounded worse than serious, but she'd already had one of the worst weeks of her life. Fate couldn't possibly be so unkind as to give her another kick in the teeth. "Now listen, you two. If this is girl stuff, that's one thing, but if we're talking about something your father should know—"

"We're not in trouble, Kat. We're not even here to talk about us," Noel jumped in. "We're here to talk about you. That it's okay with us." At Kat's blank look she waved her hands. "You know. You and Dad. It's okay."

Kat sank into the nearest, and only, spare chair. She just had the definite feeling Fate was going to give her that other kick.

"I wasn't that sure at first," Angie admitted. "I mean, like, you know, we're friends with you now. So why risk messing that up by you being a stepmother? And I worried about being loyal to Mom. Only like Noel says, Mom thought you were terrific, and it's not like Snow White and Cinderella. I mean, you're not going to change into a total different person if you become a stepmother, are you?''

Kat didn't have time to respond before Noel earnestly leaned forward. ''And Dad's been completely different since you've been around. He's got a smile on. He isn't so dead serious. It's like he's Dad again, you know?''

''He's talking and yelling and being with us again,'' Angie affirmed.

Kat tried to interrupt, but again didn't have the chance.

''And we know why.'' Noel flipped back a curl. ''We're not blind; we can both see what's been going on. And we just want you to know that you don't have to worry about us, we're here to help you. We're on your side. Dad's, too, but see...'' She shared glances with her sister. ''We're not all that sure Dad knows what he's doing.''

Angie, too naive to have guile, said, ''We're not all that sure you do, either. Maybe you think I'm only a kid, but I've picked up plenty of pointers from TV.''

''You don't do half as much with makeup as you could, Kat,'' Noel said gently.

''And Dad doesn't know what he's supposed to do, like dancing and flowers and stuff. Noel says you're probably going to have to give him a push.''

''It's been a long time for him,'' Noel said meaningfully.

''Whoa.''

''We figured we could give you a few ideas, help you arrange some things. I could cook, Angie found some candles.''

''Whoa,'' Kat repeated. She took a long look at the two hopeful, enthusiastic faces and did her best to recover from a galloping heart attack. If she had the time, she'd have raced for the library to devour a book on the raising of precocious teenage girls. Unfortunately there was no time. "First, ladies. You two are coming—totally—from left field. I'm friends with you, and, I hope, friends with your father."

"Yes, Kat."

"Yes, Kat."

"Second. I have had absolutely nothing to do with any change you see in your father. *Nothing.*"

"Yes, Kat."

"Yes, Kat." But the sisters shared a look.

"Third. I may love you two to beat the band, but that doesn't mean certain subjects aren't off-limits, even between friends. What goes on between a man and a woman is between the man and the woman. That goes for me, that goes for your father, that goes for whoever your father is involved with, now, tomorrow, or ten years from now. You do not interfere in what's none of your business. *Capisci?*"

"Yes, Kat."

"Yes, Kat."

"Fourth..." She shook her head in frustration. "You two have totally misread the situation. I'm not marrying your father. I am not going to be your stepmother. Your dad and I enjoy being together as neighbors and casual friends. That's it. Are we clear?"

"Yes, Kat."

"Yes, Kat."

The girls got a tour of the shop, handfuls of meringue cookies, a chance to try on Victorian straw hats with streaming ribbons and to play with the miniatures in the dollhouse. Eventually Kat called and paid for their taxi home. She'd thought she'd done quite well, until Noel patted her hand on the way out.

"If Dad doesn't come home tonight, I'll make Angie breakfast," she whispered. "Don't you worry about a thing. I'm old enough to understand."

Georgia found her in the office a half hour later, pulling out the hairpins that held up her pompadour and throwing them at the wall like darts. Georgia extended her palm to reveal two pellets of aspirin. Her other hand held a glass of ice water.

Kat slugged down both aspirin. "That's it," she said, and then gulped down three-quarters of the ice water. "I'm going to move. Skip town. I can't handle them and I can't handle him, and that's that."

"You want some advice?"

"Good grief, no. Advice won't help me. A case of flu before five o'clock tonight, now *that* would help me." She automatically scooped up the girls' plates and the lemonade pitcher.

"Kat, I hate to be the one to tell you this—"

"Then don't, please. Nothing good ever follows 'I hate to be the one to tell you this.'"

"But if you don't want to go out this evening, you don't need a case of flu as an excuse. You have an out. You always did. A simple, honest one."

"Heavens, what?"

"You say no," Georgia drawled. "And since you haven't exercised that option all morning, and apparently aren't going to this afternoon, you must, very much, want to be with him."

"Look, Georgia, if you can't offer anything better than insane, irrational and convoluted reasoning, I would appreciate it if you'd get back to work."

Georgia thought that was very funny, but Kat sank in her desk chair once her office was finally empty. Without ever asking a question, Georgia had managed a perceptive grasp of the situation, but not perceptive enough.

Kat hadn't canceled the five o'clock with Mick tonight because she intended to keep the date, and had known that all day. Face-to-face was the only way she could straighten out the mess she had so selfishly made.

She had told Mick that she was frigid, but she hadn't told him what mattered: that the relationship was hopeless. That she was hopeless, as a woman, mate and lover.

She took the last hairpin from her pompadour and threw it at the wall. After Todd, she'd hurt. But not like this. Todd didn't have two arrogant, pushy daughters who Kat loved like the dickens. And Todd hadn't been Mick.

Whom she loved from the soul.

If she didn't hurt so much, so hard, so fiercely, she would undoubtedly cry. How could she have been so stupid as to let Mick come to mean the whole world to her?

Mick hadn't bought rubbers since he was a teenager. Then, the little packets had been hidden from sight under the pharmacist's counter. The pharmacist was always busy, so to get them you had to face a woman—it was *always* a woman—and she *always* repeated the whispered request to the entire store in a voice louder than a tuba.

He could still remember feeling like an immoral slink, still remember the taste of guilt. Mentally he thanked God that he was an adult and times had changed.

Holding a tube of toothpaste in one hand and a bottle of mouthwash in the other, he was standing near the paper towels. The household was out of paper towels, so he had every reason to be here. It was just accidental that he was tall enough to see over the display into the condom aisle.

Times had definitely changed.

Good Lord, there were millions of them! All he remembered was two different brands. Those companies still existed but they'd expanded their repertoire so to speak. You could buy them by the packet, by the box, by the stack. You could buy them lubricated, nonlubricated, ribbed or rippled. You could buy them scented, and you could buy them colored. You could also mix and match.

He kept looking. He couldn't see a plain old basic model to save his life, and he sure as hell couldn't picture himself rolling on a fluorescent-yellow prophylactic that smelled like bananas.

"Why, Mick Larson! I see your girls all the time, but hardly ever run into you."

Faster than a thief, he clutched a double roll of paper towels before turning to face his neighbor. The last time he'd seen Mrs. Pincher, she'd been herding his two girls along with her three into a station wagon for a school play. Then, she'd had a frizzy head of brown hair turning gray, worn eyes and a maternal smile. She hadn't changed. There was no escaping her kindly meant chitchat, and she didn't begin to wear down until she'd commented on the heat spell, Harv's newest promotion and how fast all the girls were growing up. "So you're stuck shopping?"

"We were completely out of paper towels."

She tch-tched, glancing at the roll in his hands. "Those cost $1.39. Didn't you see the ones on sale up there?"

Mick obediently looked. "No, thanks a lot."

"No problem. Now don't be making yourself such a stranger, hear? One of these nights, you come over and have a beer with Harv."

"I'll do that," he promised her. She smiled and left him. Mick would have completely forgotten her if her squeaky cart hadn't turned down the condom aisle. His eyes narrowed. Ambling casually, as blithe as you please, she plucked a box off the shelf and rolled off with her cart.

So that was how it was done now. The men copped out and sent the women.

And they said women were smarter than men.

You're mentally dawdling, Larson. Move your buns. Juggling towels, mouthwash, and toothpaste, he made a U-turn into the aisle with the limitless display. The embarrassment dragging at him was abruptly shelved. His choice was, after all, a serious business, and one that affected Kat.

He hadn't had protection on the island. He hadn't expected to need it—not with the girls along, not until Kat felt more sure of the relationship—but he'd known the issue was coming. He hadn't asked if she was on the pill. There was no need to. She hadn't been involved, therefore, she wasn't likely to be prepared. That left the responsibility for birth control on him, assuming he wanted to protect her. Which he did. And assuming they were going to be sexually involved.

Which they were.

But not like the last time.

At the checkout counter, he laid down his purchases and fished for his wallet. He frowned vaguely at the checkout boy, his mind now totally focused on Kat and the evening ahead.

All week she'd done a good job of avoiding him. He understood: she'd been upset that night on the beach. So had he. There was nothing strictly wrong with a deserted beach bathed in moonlight as a romantic setting, but rough sand was not ideal for the first time. Not with Kat.

He was amazed that she'd had him fooled all these years. The flashy sports car, the flaunty walk, the hint of just a little female arrogance when she lifted one beautifully arched brow a certain way. Kat was her own woman, and she shouted it with every aspect of her life-style. Mick respected the gutsy streak, but it was the shy, vulnerable, fragile heart that he'd fallen in love with.

She had some definite inhibitions and a foolish Victorian modesty about discussing sex. Mick liked both qualities, because they showed she didn't take intimacy casually. The guy who'd hurt her was undoubtedly part of that. What mattered, though, was that long before the weekend on the island, Mick had known certain elements were critical to their first time making love. Guaranteed privacy. A comfortable setting without distractions. And a man who kept total control, not lost it.

He'd blown all three.

To a point he'd had to forgive himself. It took two to tango, and Kat took a tango with him to limits that endangered a man's central nervous system. Mick couldn't help that.

But he thought he'd known himself as a lover. He had never once doubted that once he had her beneath him, it would be good. He wasn't unselfish in bed and he knew a woman's body. A man couldn't be married fourteen years without being well aware of the uniqueness of the feminine species. A woman, for example, could change moods and become distracted faster than the flip of a dime. A man wooed her back, if he knew what he was doing.

June used to have the embarrassingly annoying habit of telling the whole neighborhood that he knew what he was doing.

He hadn't known what he was doing with Kat. Sand or no sand, he hadn't sensed her change of mood. Surf or no surf, he'd been positive she'd been as wild and willing to make love as he'd been. Her hands had helped shuck his jeans. Her eyes had the fire of impatience. His name had been on her lips, calling, whispering, demanding. Right up until the precise moment he'd slid inside her.

Dammit, what had he done wrong?

And double dammit, a lover worth his salt should know what had gone wrong, and made sure it never happened in the first place.

A blast of heat hit him the moment he strode out of the drugstore. The inside of his truck was like an oven. He threw his packages on the seat and climbed in. Clouds drifting in from the west weren't coming in fast enough. The whole city was praying for a storm to break this merciless heat wave.

Mick felt a similar frustration. Flipping the key, he cranked on his truck engine. Kat was past getting under his skin; she was tucked under his heart. With her and only with her, he'd tasted the promise of a woman who needed him. At a certain level Mick had always lived with loneliness. Kat had made the mistake of showing him it didn't have to be that way.

Tonight. It was the only word in his head. He guessed Kat was already building a mountain of nerves about the evening ahead. She had reason to be nervous.

But not for the reasons she thought.

Seven

Kat heard the rap on the door at ten minutes to five, and took one last quick look in the mirror. Since "boat shoes" had been in the invitation, she'd built an outfit around casual. Real casual. Her white cotton jeans were baggy, her navy tunic voluminous, and her oldest white tennies had floppy laces. She'd braided her hair with a red scarf and scrubbed her face—no makeup. No makeup, no scent, no jewelry.

It wasn't that she wanted to look unattractive, but she knew what she was facing tonight. Cross purposes summed it up. She had to tell him she was hopeless as a lover and make him believe it. Mick clearly hadn't been scared off after the night on the beach. Kat was terribly afraid he had something in mind along the lines of wine, music and a candlelight dinner. Her dreadful appearance had to help deter that kind of mood, and her mirror image promised her that a sex-starved hermit wouldn't look at her twice.

As satisfied as she could be, she tripped down the stairs and pulled open the front door just as Mick was about to rap a second time. Right off, something tilted in her preconceptions of the evening.

Mick wasn't exactly dressed like Mr. Seducer. He was wearing worn jeans and a short-sleeved ragged sweatshirt that flattened against his chest in the wind. His blond head was rumpled and he'd shaved, but not since morning. He took one look at her and wolf whistled. "Don't you look sexy." She didn't have to worry about Mick. He was clearly out of his mind. "Thank heavens you didn't go fancy on me, Red." He dropped a kiss on her mouth that jammed all the air in her lungs, then lifted his head and grinned. "But no more of that. This is a working dinner, and we don't have any time for dawdling."

She could see that. Mr. Chivalrous bounded down the steps ahead of her and headed for—not his sleek, quiet T-bird—but his dusty pickup. He called "Hop in!" in lieu of opening her door, and it was a good thing she was fast, because they were on the road before she'd had the chance to click her seat-belt buckle.

Kat thought fleetingly that if Mick was in a mood to seduce her, she'd eat crickets. How could she not start to relax? "What is this about a working dinner?" she demanded.

"Not all work, just some. We're going to a christening. The baby's a thirty-two footer, just a small-keeled yacht, more for pleasure than racing, but she's beautiful. I put her in the water this afternoon for the first time, but she hasn't been out yet. Her owner's in

Maine; he's hoping to hear by tomorrow how she did on this trial run. You and I are about to find out, but I'm afraid I have to make a quick detour to the shop first.''

"Shop?" she echoed. "You mean where you build your boats?"

"You don't mind, do you? It'll only take two seconds."

It took more than an hour, during which Kat was both deserted and ignored. Another woman might have felt miffed. Kat was delighted. The tense, traumatic evening she'd envisioned was fast going down the tubes. Yes, sooner or later, she had to talk to him, but it wasn't Mick's fault that he momentarily had his hands full. And it wasn't her fault that she was insatiably curious. What better way to understand a man than through his work?

Hands stuffed into her pockets, Kat poked and prodded, ambled and explored.

His "shop" was really three buildings, all white framed and as big as barns. One building stored wood. In the second, three men and Mick surrounded a huge, half-built boat; they were talking "bulkheads" and something about a "planking process." Although Mick called her over, Kat could immediately see that she was in the way.

She wanted to be in no one's way, and wandered through the third building alone and happily. This was Mick's world. Her nose crinkled because of the unfamiliar smells of acetone, lacquer thinner and varnish, even though two giant exhaust fans constantly moved air through the long, bare center of the room. She recognized power tools like a bench grinder and circular saw. Others were not familiar to her. The whole space under the rafters held templates and one long set of wall brackets provided storage for mast making. She would have known neither if they hadn't been labeled.

The labels didn't mean a thing to her, anyway. Kat couldn't pretend to know beans about boat building, but she knew what it took to run a small, independent business. Everywhere she looked she saw organization, order and control. She understood the long hours it had taken Mick to build this, and in all three buildings she could almost taste the love—the intense, unspoken, private love of a man for his work.

Mick found her just outside, perfectly content exploring his work yard. "That wasn't supposed to take so long." He was obviously upset that it had. He strode toward her with an exasperated frown and a dirt spot on his chin. "We're getting out of here."

"Are you sure you're done? You don't have to worry about me; I'm having a great time."

"I'm sure we're leaving, if we tiptoe out of here before Josh finds me to tell me another problem. When we turn the corner on the building, you race like hell for the truck and don't look back even if someone yells 'fire.'"

She chuckled. "Which one was Josh?"

"The one with the silly looking beard and lovesick eyes who looked you over good and hard when you walked in." Mick helped her into the truck. "As did the other boys." Once installed on his side, he had to lift up to dig the truck key out of his pocket. The movement tightened his jeans over the masculine bulge under the zipper. The grin he shot her was just as male. "You're lucky you snuck out of there when you did. If you had stayed any longer, the boys would've undoubtedly treated you to a five, six-hour discussion on how boats are built—or anything else they could have thought up to keep your attention."

"Everything I saw had my attention. How many boats do you build in a year? What kinds? And I take it you construct them all right inside those buildings?"

"Slow down there, Red. One question at a time."

He didn't drive toward the Charleston Harbor but toward the Ashley River, and he took Broad Street as if he knew she loved the look of the old elegant homes. Kat did, but her attention never strayed from Mick tonight.

A hot breeze vacuumed through the truck, ruffling his hair. Sunshine tipped in, accenting the lifelines and the hard, masculine planes of his face, but his voice was as shy and excited as a boy's. It was the shyness that touched Kat's heart. How long had it been since he'd felt free to share the love of his work?

He built yachts, ketches, sloops, cruisers. "Hell, I've built more than one canoe in my time. Building boats was what I wanted to do from the time I was knee-high, and I never cared what kind." The pleasure boats he specialized in usually took him a full year to build. Customers found him rather than the other way around. "Word gets around for the obvious reason. There aren't that many craftsmen who work only with wood."

He'd never anticipated growing bigger than a one-man show, but he'd doubled his work load after June died. "I thought I could handle it, until I started to realize what was happening with Noel and Angie. So about four months ago I took on Josh, who's from Boston, and Walker, he's from Savannah. A couple of apprentices make up the rest of the team." He gave her a sidelong look. "The whole crew threatens to quit once a week. They claim I'm a fussbudgety perfectionist who's impossible to please."

"They know you pretty well, hmmm?"

"Hey, whose side are you on?"

His, she thought fleetingly. A month ago, his daughters had labeled him a granite-faced sobersides. Now it wasn't animation and purpose that lightened his strong features as much as it was a building joy of life again. *You can't love him,* she told herself fiercely. But by the minute, those sensible voices in her head were growing weaker. "You browbeat your customers as bad as your employees?" she asked teasingly.

"My customers have a lot of money or they couldn't afford me, so that problem's out of the way right up front. Beyond that, my terms are real easy. We do it my way or we don't do it." He scratched his whiskered chin. "Whoops. I guess that sounded arrogant."

"A tad," she murmured dryly.

This time he frowned for real. "I've got boats in the water from the Maine to the Florida coast. They may have another owner's name on them, but they're still mine. How can I not care?"

"I understand," she murmured, and did. Mick was incapable of not caring. "You only work with wood?"

"Right."

"So what's the best wood to build a boat out of?"

Mick chuckled. "Now there's a question you could take through history and never get an answer. The old Romans would have told you silver fir; the Vikings swore by oak; ancient Egyptians favored cedar. The

Chinese have always liked a pine known as sha-mu, when they couldn't get teak."

"No one agrees what's best?"

"Sure, there's agreement. Any practical boat builder would tell you that there are high-quality, tropical hardwoods available today: utile, iroko, opepe. It's only your bullheaded purists who still hold out for teak, oak and mahogany."

"So what do you build with?"

He looked surprised that she'd asked. "Teak, oak and mahogany. Or I don't build."

She intended to rib him about the "bullheaded purist" nonsense, until they reached the docks. Late-afternoon sun glinted with crystal brilliance on the bobbing boats in the harbor. Kat didn't know a ketch from a sloop but she guessed, on sight, which one was his—the incomparable beauty with the blinding white paint, the gleam of varnished teak deck, the sleek and elegant lines. *You do realize how hopelessly biased you've become, Bryant?*

But she was right. Mick headed down the grassy slope, onto the wooden plank dock, past beautiful boat on beautiful boat, but he stopped at the one that had captured her attention. Not that he loved the thirty-two-foot baby, but he paused to look for a minute with his hands on his hips and his heart in his eyes.

Darn man. Kat had promised herself that she would stay physically out of reach all evening, but Mick just wasn't giving her a choice. She slid an arm around his waist and hugged him, hard. "You love her."

He squeezed back, just as hard. "Yeah."

"So keep her, Mick. Can't you?"

"Sure, I could. I could give the guy back his money or build him another one. The problem with that is that I get this blasted attached to every one I build." His hand slid down her spine to her fanny, and patted hard. "And what's to keep? For all I know she's going to sink on the high seas, assuming we ever get her out there. And you're about to work for your dinner. Your first job is letting go of the lines."

"Okay by me." She immediately and enthusiastically took off.

"Ah, Red?"

"What?"

"You might want to save the last line until we're on board?" He pushed his sunglasses on top of his head and grinned. "Real seasoned sailor, hmmm?"

"Are we going to sail her?"

He leaped on board first, then reached for her hand. "Not on this trial run. I want to check out her engine, see how she feels and responds in the water. You're going to have your hands just as full. I need everything checked out below deck that can be, and not like a boat builder would do it but like a woman would."

"If you're trying to tell me my place is in the kitchen, Larson—"

"Galley." He shoved a mate's cap on her head and grinned. "You're going to have to get this lingo down. The bathroom's called a head; the beds are called berths. Then there's fore..." He tapped his forefinger to the tip of her breasts. "Aft..." He cupped her fanny. "And while I'm on board you're supposed to call me 'captain,' but hey, I'm not fussy. I'll settle for a respectful 'sir.'"

"You'll settle in the deep six if you keep this up. How's that for a nautical term?"

"Impressive." He would have kissed her, but she wouldn't stand still.

As far as Mick could tell, Kat took to sailing like she took to everything else, passionately and with total enthusiasm. Within fifteen minutes he was steering the boat down the Ashley River toward the Charleston Harbor, which was a tricky business, since both were dominated by shallows and sandbar islands. The wind had picked up, intensifying the sea smells, and the current was strong.

Kat was everywhere: hanging over the rail for a glimpse of the huge white mansions on Charleston's shoreline, then nimble footed exploring the foredeck, where the waves splashed in her face and made her laugh. She demanded a thorough explanation of every gauge and meter on the control console, then bounded below deck to explore the cabin. She spent fifteen minutes there before he saw her head peeking through the open hatch. "I just thought I'd better tell you. You're keeping her, Mick. You're just going to have to tell that poor klutz in Maine that he's out of luck."

"Like her, do you?"

"Like? What kind of word is that? I'm talking love; I'm talking grand passion."

She was still crowing when she disappeared from sight. He hauled her back up to see a school of dolphins, then to see a covey of sandhill cranes that had sought sanctuary on one of the mini wild islands that dotted the harbor. It didn't take long for the wind to destroy any semblance of neatness to her braid. Tendrils whipped around her nape and brow. Her cheeks picked up a breeze-whipped coral. He pelted out an occasional order just to see the saucy grin on her face.

All he could think of was that this was what he'd wanted for her, this was what he had planned. When he'd first picked her up, Kat had been so wary, so sure she was being set up for a seduction scene. She'd been right to be nervous . . . and wrong.

In these hours together, he'd wanted her to see that they were a natural pair. She was happy with him. The differences between them—she was lace and cameos, he was a physical man who would always work with his hands—were superficial. He didn't have to understand Victorian corsets or gridwork to respect what it took her to manage a business. She didn't have to understand the technicalities in building a boat to share his love for what he did.

He'd wanted to tease Kat—all right, he wanted to seduce her—with the kind of life they would have together.

Past the harbor, in a cove where the waves softly swelled and the sun was just starting to set in rainbow prisms over the water, he cut the engine and dropped anchor. His "baby," on her maiden run, had proven responsive and sensitive to his slightest touch on her throttle. Any skipper knew that patience and experience paid off at the helm.

As a man, he'd forgotten those very good rules with Kat. When they got around to making love, Mick was now prepared. Tonight, though, he had in mind loving her well and thoroughly, but not physically. In a dozen ways she'd told him she was wary of sex. Kat needed time, and Mick was a man of patience, control and experience, which he intended to prove to her if it killed him.

He thought of her mouth, the dance of sunlight in her eyes. And mentally groaned just before heading below deck.

Kat was in trouble and knew it when he served dinner. From the moment he'd picked her up, Mick had sabotaged her nervous, careful, cautious mood. She'd tried to stay nervous, but it just wasn't working. She'd tried to stay tense, but he'd made it impossible for her not to relax. And she'd worked up a reasonably healthy head of anxiety about their one-on-one dinner.

That died the moment Mick set down a steaming, messily overflowing platter of crawfish, then a fragrant, spicy dish of red beans and rice. "We're going to need a million napkins, and what do you want to drink? Iced tea? A beer?"

"Beer, please, but I'll get it." She twisted tops off two bottles and carried them back to the table. Her fears of candlelight and seduction scenes seeming sillier by the minute, she swung a leg under her and ravenously dived into the ethnic food. "You're going to have to eat fast to keep up with me," she warned him. "I haven't had crawfish in a hundred years."

Mick didn't feel obligated to mention that his daughters had clued him in to Kat's favorite foods. "Some people wouldn't mind that lag in time."

"Some people don't appreciate Southern coast cooking."

"I think you have your geography a little confused. This food's strictly Louisiana Bayou, hardly South Carolina coast."

"Who's picky? South is South. And how much red pepper did you put in the beans?"

He didn't answer that, just brought the spice container to the table with a grin. "When you burn your tongue, I'll have a second beer handy, and I can't wait to see how the lady tackles the etiquette of eating crawdads."

"The only etiquette that applies in this case is enthusiasm." Manners didn't work. There was nothing messier than digging into a platter of crawfish. She broke off a tail, poked her thumbs in the ridge of the shell to split it, then used her fingers to pull out the succulent white meat. The first taste was bliss. The second was even better.

Mick drawled, "Is this by any chance your first meal in weeks, Red?"

"Go ahead and make fun. You're denting that platter as fast as I am." And he was having a wonderful time doing it, she thought fleetingly. When had she ever heard Mick laugh this much? Or forget all his stress and just be happy?

"I was going to ask you how the checklist went on the cabin, but I've changed my mind. It would obviously be too taxing for you to talk and eat at the same time."

She ignored that insult, since to respond was to encourage more teasing. But her hand waved expansively around the cabin. "I checked out all the appliances and what-alls on your list, which was a total waste of time. You had to know everything's perfect. Beyond perfect."

"You think so?"

As they continued to eat, Kat's gaze prowled the cabin. Everything was teak and teal-blue, richness and comfort.

The main cabin was luxurious. The open galley was tiny, but more fully equipped than her own kitchen. The U-shaped dinette faced a couch cushioned with thick, fat teal-blue cushions. Above the navigational desk was a compact entertainment system. She couldn't see the head from where she was sitting, but if she craned her neck she could glimpse the edge of the water-blue comforter on the raised double berth in the "bedroom."

Boats were Mick's world, not hers. Yet because they were Mick's world, it was easy to imagine a honeymoon on a boat like this. Making love, sailing the seas, waking to the rhythm of sleepy waves and making love all over again. Kat's eyes suddenly squeezed closed.

"You're not giving up already?" Mick scolded.

She forced a smile as she pushed aside her plate. "I'm shamefully full now."

"But you only ate enough for three men, Red. I was sure you could do better than that."

She roused the energy to toss a wadded napkin at him. It didn't make it halfway across the table, which was, not surprisingly, a disastrous mess. "All right, Larson, you're all done playing boss. Close your eyes and put your feet up," she ordered him. "I'll take care of this."

"We will," he corrected her.

"There isn't enough room in the galley for two. Besides, I can do it twice as fast alone."

He wouldn't listen. Every time Kat turned around, she was bumping into Mick. Her thigh brushed his when she bent over the silverware drawer. His arm grazed her shoulder when he reached to put away a glass. Desire hummed between them, as unspoken as moonlight, as familiar and potent as the growing love she felt for him.

Outside, starlight filtered in the open portholes. When the moon had come up, the wind had died. The Atlantic was out there, the whole night smelled of a moon-drenched ocean, and Kat kept telling herself to get real, get tough and face up to what she had to say. Loving Mick didn't make any difference. She wasn't normal. She wasn't like other women. No relationship was possible.

Only she couldn't seem to believe that when she was with him. She felt no more, no less and no different than any other woman in love. She didn't want so much. Just the right to other nights like this, nights when she bumped into him in a kitchen, nights when they ate dinner in bare feet, nights when she put up with his teasing and she was so damned happy she forgot that her hair was a tangled mess.

Mick never cared what a woman's hair looked like. All he wanted in this life was someone he could share with. Although he'd never criticized June, Kat understood something had been missing in the relationship, something he'd felt guilty for wanting, something he'd felt badly for needing.

There was no guilt in need, no shame in weakness. He was weakest where he loved most, his daughters, his work. He didn't seem to understand that that didn't make him less, but more, of a man.

She'd tried, by listening and being there, to coax him out of his shell. She knew she'd helped, only it suddenly, painfully occurred to her that she had never had a way to tell Mick how much she thought of him as a man.

When she folded the dish towel, Mick was just turning from where he had been storing a tray in a closet. "Are there still things you need to do on the boat?" she asked him.

"Not really. I have a list to take back to the shop tomorrow morning, but it's just little fix-it things. Nothing I need to handle now." Mick's hand was halfway to an itch on the back of his neck when his heart stopped beating. Kat took a step toward him, which didn't have to mean anything at all except that she was moving away from the galley. There was just something in her eyes. "On the ride back, I have a few things to do. She's well equipped for night runs, but I put an extra safety package on her that I'd like to—"

His heart restarted. But with a pound, not a beat. Kat wasn't walking by him but coming to him. When her arms roped around his neck, blood slushed through his veins in a rush of heat. When her lips lifted to his and connected, he felt a loss of balance.

He tasted good. A little spice, a little beer, a little Mick. He was awkwardly tall to kiss when she wasn't wearing shoes. Leverage was only possible on tiptoe. Leverage didn't concern her. His mouth did. Reaching it, savoring it, exploring it.

She already knew that Mr. Larson liked kissing. She'd had no idea how much he loved being kissed. Amazing, how quiet it suddenly was in the cabin. All she could hear was the distant splash of sleepy waves and the low—wild and low—groan in the back of his throat when she kissed him again.

"Ah, Red?"

"Hmmm?" Her smile was brazen, calm, confident. He'd never know she was more scared than a kitten in a tree. She unwound her arms and let her hands slide down to the bottom of his sweatshirt. The material raveled around her wrist as her palms glided back up. His blond chest hair curled around her fingers, and his flesh was supple and warm. Very warm. Far too warm for him to need the sweatshirt.

"Is this all to tell me you liked the crawfish?"

"No, Mick. This is for you." It's all she had to say for that arrogant smile of his to fade, but he didn't move. She knew what he wanted. She'd known what he wanted all evening—the one thing she couldn't give him—but that need was in his eyes now, flaring hotter than blue fire. He delivered the dare, just not verbally. *If you want it, babe, you're gonna have to come and get it. I'm not going to push you.*

She pulled the sleeve of his sweatshirt off one arm. Then the other.

When his sweatshirt was in a nice little puddle on the floor, she framed his face between her hands and raised on tiptoe again. Her tongue moved over his bottom lip, lazy and slow. She nipped, whisper light.

And then she took his mouth as though she'd die if she couldn't have it.

He liked that kiss. A lot. Every muscle coiled in his body like a single-loaded spring. She sampled his tongue with her tongue. He liked that, too. He liked the feel of her palms climbing up the warm, smooth skin of his spine; he liked the way her soft pelvis rubbed right where he was hard...and Kat told herself that she was nuts.

Only she didn't feel nuts. She felt a trembling deep inside. It had been her fault he'd felt badly about the night on the beach. He was a beautiful, powerful, virile lover. Putting a definite end to the relationship—Kat had no choice. But it suddenly mattered terribly that she first show him how she felt about him, how she saw him, how much he meant to her.

And there was only one way to do that.

"We can make love, Mick," she whispered. "Just not . . . regular . . . love."

"Regular?"

He didn't seem real involved in the conversation so she persevered. "I have to be honest, okay?"

"Sweetheart, you just don't get much more honest than this." Sometime during the last kiss—or the ten before it—he'd loosened her braid and freed the red silk scarf from the tangled plait. His mouth crushed hers, and when his tongue drove inside, a roar filled her ears like the sound of a waterfall.

"I . . . need you to listen."

He claimed he was, in between stringing a pearl of kisses down the length of her throat. Those kisses were destroying her concentration, but maybe that was just as well. If it were any man but Mick, she'd never have managed this at all.

"This has to be just for you . . . I . . ." The words weren't coming out, but she was sure he understood. She wasn't naive. Hey, there were other ways to please a man besides missionary positions and penetration. ". . . I know of two. Only I've never done one, Mick, and the other . . . I'm just saying I might need some help, okay?"

Somewhere between kisses and gulped whispers, she seemed to have caught his attention. He raised his head. When had his eyes turned that piercing, fierce blue? With intense concentration, he brushed her kiss-swollen bottom lip with the pad of his thumb. And then he smiled. A slow, sure, man's smile, so wicked they would have banned it in Boston.

Her knees turned to rubber. His mouth dropped back on hers again and his hands shifted, sliding down her spine to cup her bottom. He lifted her, winding her legs around his waist without ever breaking the kiss, and carried her through the carved arch to the back cabin.

She landed on the thick comforter with a whoosh. He landed on her, not with his full weight but enough of it. He was aroused.

The back cabin was dark. Courage came from the darkness, from determination, from the power of her emotions. At least it started out that way. Kat knew exactly what she wanted to do—make him feel loved and desired and beautiful as a man. Bold like she'd never been bold, she spread kisses like confetti on his mouth, throat, shoulders, chest. Brazen like she'd never been brazen, she rubbed her palms down his side, rimmed the waistband of his jeans, splayed her fingers on the hard ridge of his hips.

He liked what she did—his response left her no doubt—only Mick stopped cooperating. She'd done her best to explain that this had to be her ball game, only he wasn't helping at all. Her tunic was loose, making it easy for his callused hand to slip inside. The tip of his thumb traced the lace rim of her bra. She felt a nasty sensation, like falling out of the sky.

"Mick—"

"Sssh." He lifted her as delicately as if she were a spring flower...but he tugged off her navy-blue tunic and hurled it away like unwanted baggage. He didn't seem to think much more of her best lilac, lace-edged bra. A zillion degrees Fahrenheit, the humidity worse, and her bare nipples suddenly puckered as though she was freezing. He ducked his head.

His tongue had a way with a nipple. She arched for the teasing spear of his tongue, then felt his teeth. She was small, and flat on her back she was certainly smaller. His palms cupped both breasts, giving him something to lave, tease, torment, lick. She couldn't catch her breath. She couldn't stop her heart from pounding.

Rolling over him, her hair falling like a curtain around her face, she kissed him. A wet kiss this time. A wet, openmouthed, wanton kiss, because, dammit, he was asking for it. "Mick..."

"You're unbearably beautiful, love."

The man was not himself. "I wish you wouldn't do that."

"You love it when I do that."

"But this is supposed to be for you." She found the button on his jeans. Her voice dropped an octave when she slid down the zipper, and her voice hadn't been all that high to begin with. Mick didn't wear skintight jeans. It was just now they were fitting that way. "I thought you understood. I want to..." Her fingers slid under the waistband and tugged down. "I need to...I want to...Mick, I—"

"Red, it can't be all that hard to tell me you want my jeans off." He kicked the last of his clothes free, and kissed her mouth with a smile. A smile loaded in the darkness with TNT.

"You don't understand."

"Believe me, I do."

"Mick, I want to please you."

"You do that by breathing."

"I mean just you." Dammit. His tongue was on her neck, melting her collarbone, at the same time his knuckles were pulling at her jeans zipper. "It won't work any other way. And I don't care. I don't need anything for me. I just want—''

He had to lift her up to pull off her jeans, then the bare strip of violet lace panties. He never looked at the clothes, just at her face, her eyes. "This time, just this time," he said softly, "I want you to trust me to know what you want. Stop worrying, Kat. I love you, don't you know that?''

"I—"

"I'd sworn I wouldn't let this happen. Not tonight. I'd sworn I was going to give you all the time you wanted, but the look in your eyes, honey...time is not what you're asking me for.''

She tried to say something else. "Sssh," he murmured, and came back down to her, bare skin against bare skin, kisses tangling in a fast unraveling skein. It seemed to have taken him forever to interpret her desperately low mumblings to mean that she had the cockamamy idea of getting him off and not her.

If she thought he'd buy that, he had an island in Iowa he wanted to sell her. Tomorrow.

Not now. Right now there was only one thing on Mick's mind. Kathryn was scared, he knew, but not half as scared as she thought. Her eyes were sleepy with passion, her limbs winding around his, her small white breasts so swollen they had to hurt her. This time Mick was sure. This time there'd be no bungling his precious cargo. Her mouth yielded more than passion under his. The tension building in her lower body sought release from more than the physical.

She wanted to be loved.

His mouth claimed hers as his palm traced her inner thigh, then cupped the soft protective moss between her legs. She was damp, and bucked around his hand, trying to draw him closer at the same time her teeth nipped his lip. He stroked and kissed until her nails dented the skin on his back, but Mick ignored those messages. There was a time for a pell-mell rush into passionate oblivion, and a time for that wicked country ballad about slow hands.

This was a time for slow hands.

She loved the music. She loved the music so much he nearly went out of his mind—but didn't. Nothing was going wrong this time, because he wasn't going to let it. Lord, she was beautiful, all sweetness and silk and scent and need . . .

"Mick."

Damn tinfoil. He kissed her the whole time he was rolling on the condom. As it happened, she wouldn't have noticed if it were fluorescent yellow or plain. She didn't care. Her eyes were glazed, as lost as a kitten's, and she wasn't playing at brazen now. She wanted, and her feverish kisses were filled with the wonder of that; awkward then sweet, wanton then impatient. It was as if she'd stored up desire for the past ten years, stored up love to shower over him, and he sure as hell wasn't going to disappoint her.

He repositioned his thighs over her thighs, her soft cries driving him as much as the fierce trust in her eyes, the passion in her hands. As if he enjoyed torture, he hesitated at the entrance. Not for long. He wasn't made of steel. Just long enough to savor how good, how right, how erotic he felt. And how much he loved her.

"Please, Mick. . . ."

He intruded that slick, warm velvet, and felt his heart climb out of his chest. He heard her call his name, again, again.

And then again, this time differently.

She'd been as wet as a river. He knew it. He'd felt it.

Only now she was suddenly as dry as a drought in the Sahara, and the moisture in her eyes wasn't a glaze of passion but tears.

Eight

Mick withdrew, clamped his jaws together and fought for control. A triple shot of bourbon might have helped him. There was an alliterative locker-room phrase starting with "blue" that described his immediate physical condition. Desire didn't want to die. Wanting her refused to go away. She didn't help matters when she squirmed.

"Just where do you think you're going, Kathryn?"

"I was—"

"No, you're not."

"I need to—"

"No, you don't." She was trembling, which annoyed him no end. He tucked her back where she belonged, next to him and naked where she could cause him more torture. Her face was as white as ice and her eyes squeezed closed. "Look at me."

Kat didn't want to. She wanted to click her heels three times and end up in Kansas, preferably with an assumed name and under the protection of an Auntie Em.

That choice being impossible, her lips framed an apology, but the words clogged in the lump of guilt in her throat. No apology justified putting him through this twice. Her conscience wouldn't buy the excuse that she'd only wanted to please him and had never intended their lovemaking to take the turn it had. Although that was true, she could have stopped it. There was a moment when she'd known the blind, powerful wave of desire was taking them both. She'd let it happen—for the unforgivable reason that making love with Mick had seemed the most natural thing on earth.

Once more she'd let herself believe that it had to be right with him.

Once more she'd hurt him. Being swallowed by a black hole had a lot of immediate appeal. Anything was better than opening her eyes and facing him. "Blow up if you want to, Mick." Her voice was as low as the scratch of sandpaper. "If I were a man, I'd be spitting mad."

"If I were a woman, I'd probably be spitting mad, too." That made her eyes blink open. He saw her confusion. She obviously expected him to be angry. Maybe he was, but at the situation, not at her. One look at Kat's face and tenderness tore through him. "As far as I can tell, both of us are biting the same bullet," he said quietly. "You got cheated just as badly as I did."

"That's different because it's my fault. Completely." She lurched up. "I should have told you before and I'm ashamed that I didn't. What happened shouldn't have, because I knew. I was engaged to a man named Todd five years ago; we broke up because of this, so I knew. You're talking lynching guilty from the start—I knew I had no right to become involved. Not with anyone, never with you. Please believe that I never wanted to hurt you—"

"Get back here, Red," he said calmly.

She wasn't listening. If it wasn't so dark, if her vision wasn't blurred by tears, if the boat wasn't rocking, she'd undoubtedly be able to find her tunic somewhere on the floor. She'd have settled for sack cloth. Anything to cover herself.

"There are zillions of normal women out there. You won't have any trouble finding one. The best I can say for me is that I'm a walking advertisement for safe sex. For a long time I've tried to see the humor in that. I mean, hey, I'm the safest date in town. Real funny, isn't it? Dammit, I can't talk about this. I never could, I never will, and I will thoroughly understand if you drop me in the Atlantic on the return ride home. I just—"

She was still searching for her tunic when Mick's hands closed on her waist from behind. She was redeposited flat on the bed with the ease of a sack of potatoes. Naked suddenly had a new dimension. He'd wedged her between the solid cabin wall and him. She wasn't going anywhere. His eyes were steel blue, uncompromisingly patient and inarguably determined. "No one, Kat, is laughing or thinks anything is funny. No one wants to drop you in the Atlantic, and if you ever want to see me really lose my temper, try handing me that garbage about 'not being normal' again."

His leg pinned her as securely as a manacle, but infinitely gentle, his fingers sifted through the auburn strands that clung damply to her temples. "We're going to talk."

"We just did talk." She didn't understand. "I've told you the truth. There's nothing else to say."

"Maybe on your terms. On mine, we haven't even started." His thumb brushed the last drop of moisture from her cheeks. The teardrop was almost as fragile as her mouth. Not quite. Nothing was as fragile as Kat's mouth. "I guessed you were involved with someone. A turkey. He's the one who dropped the label 'frigid' on you, wasn't he? There are no frigid women, honey, only callous lovers. I don't know whether he physically hurt you or was just damned selfish."

She shook her head. It didn't dislodge his hand. "Todd wasn't a turkey and it wasn't like that. It was just me. My problem. And I know I should have been more honest with you from the beginning."

"You are honest with me, every time I touch you, every time you respond. Washington would have given you an award for emotional honesty, sweets, it's just words that get tricky for you. So we'll work on that." He tucked a pillow under both their heads. "You told me about the fiancé, but what about before him? Maybe somebody came on to you real strong? Maybe worse than that?"

"Good heavens, no."

"You told me you were pretty wild as a teenager."

She rolled her eyes and made her voice deadpan. "I also told you that was fake. A boy named Sammy Rogers copped a feel in the school hallway when I was in seventh grade. I knocked him flat. That's my entire history of sexual scares."

"We're talking about being honest." There was warning in his tone.

"I can't talk at all. Not about this." She lifted her head. "Don't you think we should get dressed? Wouldn't you like a beer? How about if we talk about boats?"

He raised one bushy blond brow. "You wouldn't be trying to get out of this bed again, would you, Red?"

"I think a vertical conversation would be wise."

"I think that certain conversations can only take place prone."

"I don't do much of anything well when prone. That's what I've been trying to tell you. There's just nothing else to say, except that if I were you, I'd throw me off the boat. Think about it, Mick. It's good advice."

He fussed like a schoolmaster. When he was done rearranging body parts, his thigh had locked between hers, her cheek was on his chest, her head was wedged under his chin, and his arms were tightly, securely wrapped around her. "Now." There was a wealth of masculine satisfaction in his voice. She couldn't imagine why. He'd successfully rearoused yearning, lustfully active hormones that she'd been praying were dead, dead, dead. "If we can't find a problem with *you*, Kat, it's pretty obvious we have a problem with *us*."

"Not us. Me."

"Wrong. You don't have a problem, love. We do. Because that's how it is when two people love each other. You did realize that, didn't you? That you love me like hell?"

She swallowed hard. His tone was teasing, but Mick wasn't. His heartbeat thumped right under her cheek. How could she lie to him? "Yes."

"And maybe you're telling me there was no big emotional trauma that led to *our* little problem. But unless I've misunderstood one heck of a lot, we have absolutely no problem with chemistry or desire. To put it as delicately as I know how—" Mick cleared his throat "—you've kind of given me reason to believe you want me like hell."

"Lord, Mick, do you think I'd have let it go this far if I didn't? I know that's no excuse, but every time we..." She gulped. "You think it's not embarrassing that I turn on like a light switch every time you..." Her breath caught again. "For heaven's sake, I'm thirty-three years old and I haven't dated anyone in five years. Don't you think I know what control is? It's only with you that..." Her arm sprang out, trying to express what she couldn't. "That was the whole problem, why I kept letting it go on without telling you; it was just so hard for me to accept that anything could go wrong when it was you."

"Hmmm." His lips skimmed her temple. "I think you just gave me an enormous ego boost, but it's kind of hard to tell between all those 'it's' and 'anythings' and hesitations." There was a smile in his kiss, but his eyes were serious when he tilted her face to look at her. "I want you, too," he said softly. "In a way that feels out of control, in a way that feels right, so damned right it scares me. And where I come from when a man feels that strongly he doesn't turn tail and run out at the first sign of a glitch."

The emotion in his voice made her throat swell—until his last words. She choked out, "Mick! This is more than a glitch!"

"Yeah, well, we're about to come to that." He sighed, not without humor. "I know blunt and bawdy isn't exactly your style, Red, but we've talked around the problem as far as we can go. Ever had a nice, plain, explicit course in anatomy?"

She was not amused. "Come on, Mick. I mastered the birds and the bees a long time ago."

"And that's good, real good, but this time I have a little more advanced course in mind. In this anatomy course we're going to cover slightly trickier material, starting with what the thigh bone's connected to and moving on to how you work, how I work, what you like, where you like it." He wagged a finger at her. "Only I know you, Red. The rules are no euphemisms, and no fill in the blanks. Think you can manage that?"

If he wanted to know what she thought he wanted to know, that answer was easy. "No."

"Sure, you can. If it's with me. I thought you already knew there was nothing you couldn't talk to me about, and besides that we'll start out real easy." He drawled, "There's a certain whatchamacallit that's pressing real hard against your thigh at the moment. By any chance do we know the proper name for that whatchamacallit?"

"Mick!" Darn him, she was starting to laugh.

"That question too hard? Don't sweat it. This professor's prepared to cater to the class." With his brow furrowed in deep concentration, he traced the shape of her breast with the pad of his thumb. "Now this dohickey here. What do you like to call this, Red?"

There was no controlling the devil. The blunter the question, the more mercilessly he teased. If she dared turn shy, she got a big scolding about Victorian missish modesty. . . and another explicit question.

It wasn't the use of proper words that embarrassed her. Kat could certainly handle a discussion on basic biology, but there were certain things she'd never imagined sharing with a man. How could she talk about what turned her on, where she was sensitive, what physically happened to her when she made love?

Mick made it very clear that no subject was taboo between lovers. Ever. Always. Embarrassment was okay. Skimpy answers were not. Unfortunately he expected her to know more about her body than she actually did. Good grief, a busy woman had more to do in a day than analyze her bodily functions; how was she supposed to know if PMS affected her sexual responsiveness?

It had to be the most awkward, dreadful, squirmy discussion she'd ever had in her life.

Or it started out that way. Over time, starlight drifted through the porthole skylight. Over time, the boat kept rocking to the lulling, sensual rhythm of the sea. Over time, she understood exactly why she had never been able to stop herself from falling in love with Mick. What she couldn't possibly share with another living soul, she could share with him. The vulnerable part of a woman's soul that she guarded so carefully was safe with him.

Mick Larson was a man to hold, cherish, protect, love. She desperately wanted to do all those things, and at the first lull in the conversation, she lifted her head to look at him. His blond hair was disheveled. He was still lying naked—it would never occur to Mick to be self-conscious about nudity—but his face was set in grave lines.

She reached over to smooth the furrow in his brow. "Is the inquisitor finally done?" she murmured.

"No."

But she knew he'd finally run out of questions. That was why he was so unhappy. Mick had thought their talk would yield answers—a reason, a clue, a key to her problem. He'd counted on that. "I need to tell you something that we haven't discussed," she said softly. "Something . . . terribly personal, terribly private."

She had his full attention and she took advantage of it. "You are," she said quietly, "the most exciting lover I can imagine. You're not getting away with thinking that you've failed me as a lover, because you haven't. All those questions, Mick . . . but there was never anything you failed to do, no 'technique' you missed, and you already know more about a woman's anatomy than I do." She put a finger on his lips when he tried to talk.

"Every time you've touched me, you've pleased me. I've loved what you do, everything you do. There's no way it could have been better, no way you could have been more alluring as a lover. The problem is strictly mine, not yours, and so is the answer. I have to stop seeing you."

"No."

But she closed her eyes and took a long breath. "Yes."

Ed's fuzzy white head appeared in the doorway. "Rithwald's on the phone, wants to know when you're going to finish the price on the Bickford renovation."

"1999."

"Ah." Ed cleared his throat. "He was sort of counting on a week from Tuesday."

"Whatever." Ed disappeared. Kat glared at the recipe for Princess Cake clothespinned in front of her. She poured an egg, three egg yolks and three-quarters of a cup of sugar in the small mixing bowl. The mixer whined, oblivious to ringing phones, customers and Georgia's quietly hummed "Battle Hymn of the Republic." The batter spattered and swirled for a solid three minutes. When Kat switched it off, Georgia was still humming. "Would you stop it?"

"Stop what?"

"Stop humming that blasted song!"

"It seemed to suit your mood," Georgia said mildly. She glanced at the potato flour and baking soda Kat was mixing in the bowl. "You're supposed to cream the mixture, darlin'. Not beat it to death." She dipped a spoon in the stove-top double boiler. She tasted, then kept stirring. "You suppose it's been the heat affecting your mood for the past two weeks?"

"If you're implying I've been difficult to work with—"

"I think you could've given lessons to the Ayatollah," Georgia said genially.

Kat stopped stirring. "I'm sorry." She lifted her head. "Honestly sorry, Georgia."

"Forget it. You've put up with my low spots for five years; it's kind of nice to have the chance to return the favor."

"I'm not low."

"Of course, you're not."

Exasperated, Kat flipped the mixer back on to beat the egg whites. No one could talk over the sound of the mixer at its highest speed. Ed popped back in, took a wary glance at her, and popped back out. The college girl manning the store wandered through, and when Georgia shook her head, she disappeared again.

Wednesday afternoons were traditionally baking times at the store. That tradition had become possible because the building had originally housed a restaurant. The cooking facilities were ancient but functional, the customers loved the Victorian treats, and cooking was a love of Georgia's—not Kat's. Georgia couldn't remember a single Wednesday in which Kat had ever done more than sample the products.

Eventually the egg whites were peaked and glossy. The moment Kat shut off the mixer, Georgia subtly pounced. "So, are you going to New Orleans with Mick this weekend?"

Kat dropped the spoon. "Isn't anybody's private business sacred around here anymore? How did you even know he asked me?"

"Someone had to clear your schedule if you wanted to be away," Georgia said logically. "I gather he has someone named Uncle Bill to take care of the girls, but your working hours can be a little harder to rearrange."

"There's nothing to rearrange because I won't be going. Which Mick already knows." Kat folded the egg whites into the cake batter, poured the batter into the pan and put the whole thing into the oven. Thirty minutes to bake. If she had thirty minutes with nothing to do, she'd go crazy.

"I think he thinks you're going."

"That's only because he doesn't listen." She could prepare part of the topping ahead of time. Not the powdered sugar, but she could mix the food coloring for the nine-ounce roll of marzipan—assuming she could find the green coloring. Her fingers knocked over a half-dozen spice containers. Good Lord, it was hot and humid. "Mick doesn't listen. He doesn't understand the word no. He's sneaky and unprincipled. And he lies."

"I had no idea," Georgia said mildly. "To look at him, you'd think he had integrity stamped all over his face."

"Quit the humor, Georgia. I'm serious." She jammed the spice containers back in place. "He called me last Thursday morning, all upset because he'd caught Noel kissing some boy. He just wanted to have lunch and talk to me, he said." She glared at Georgia. "What was I supposed to do, ignore him? He was upset. I couldn't just . . ."

"Of course you couldn't."

"The lunch was a total setup. He'd hired a horse-drawn buggy for a drive around the harbor, set up this picnic lunch in the grass by the water, and dammit, he brought me roses."

"Now there's a loser for you," Georgia murmured obligingly.

"He lied, Georgia. He did not want to talk about Noel."

"Lynch the sucker," Georgia advised.

"You keep laughing, but you don't have the whole picture," Kat said irritably. Finally she found the green food coloring and started shaking it in the bowl. "Last Saturday night, Angie called me. She'd cooked her first dinner, entirely by herself, and she was so proud of herself she was going nuts. I could hardly hurt her feelings."

"Of course not."

"So I went over there, expecting four at the table. The menu was burned coq au vin, tepid champagne and raw broccoli. The table was set with candles and a neighbor's borrowed sterling, and the girls ran giggling out of sight the minute I got there."

"Leaving you alone with Mick?"

"He knew." Kat shook a dripping spoon at Georgia. "He let the girls set that up. He knows damn well they're becoming far too attached to me, and all he keeps saying is how they're thriving under my feminine influence, how they need me. He's deliberately encouraging the girls to believe I could be part of their lives."

"No question, the man is scum. Slime. A man who would use his own daughters—"

Kat was no longer listening to Georgia's nonsense. Her tone had turned wistful, her eyes lost. "And I'll never, never, forgive him the camellias."

"Camellias?"

"You remember Monday how busy we were? I didn't get home until late, so tired I could hardly walk. All I wanted out of life was a long soak in the bath, so I crawled upstairs and there they were. A tubful. An entire tubful of beautiful, fragile, precious white camellias." She looked helplessly at Georgia. "I love camellias."

Georgia nodded. "That man obviously has a real vicious streak. You can't get much more down and dirty than camellias."

"I can't go with him to New Orleans. I've told him no to New Orleans, no to the relationship, no to everything. I said no and I meant it, Georgia. I simply have to stay out of his life." Something was terribly wrong. The few drops of food coloring were supposed to turn the marzipan pale green. The mixture was as dark as an Amazon emerald.

Georgia glanced over. "Don't come within five feet of my cream filling, darlin'."

"I'm not."

"There's one more roll of almond paste in the refrigerator, but only one more. Maybe you'd better let me do the marzipan."

"Don't be silly. I can handle it. I know perfectly well what I have to do...." The words caught in her throat. Kat always had known what she had to do and had always done it. Until lately. Lately she couldn't seem to concentrate on her work, her life, nothing. Nothing made sense.

Blunt, practical, physical Mick had started this crazy romantic courtship when he *knew* her problem.

Camellias.

For a woman who couldn't make love.

She was going to rent that man a straitjacket. The very first day she stopped feeling so weepy.

Georgia said casually, "Wynn was his name."

"Whose name?"

"The man I was in love with. Did I ever tell you about him?"

Kat abruptly turned her head. Georgia knew perfectly well that she'd never mentioned a word about her past.

"Hmmm. He was tall and good-looking, and you can't get much more Yankee than a Vermonter. He was built on the lean side, had a little Newman in the eyes, and you know I'm a little sensitive about my weight?"

Kat nodded, feeling her heart reach out to her friend. She knew.

"Wynn wasn't. Wynn liked plump. He also liked raspberries and mint juleps and books. He had too much money for his own good. He was a Type A all day, prone to worry, didn't know how to relax. I soothed him, he used to say. He didn't soothe me. When I was around him, he stirred me up more than a fox in a hen house." Georgia shot Kat a smile. "I left him."

"Oh, sweetie, why?" Kat asked softly.

"Couldn't have children and he wanted children. He knew, said we'd make a go of it anyway, but I was afraid he'd come to resent me. So I decided to make it easier for him and call it off." Georgia stuck her finger back in the double boiler, burned it, and was satisfied the mixture was finally done. "I've had seven years to live with that decision. Seven years to reap all the rewards of doing the best thing for Wynn."

It didn't look that way to Kat. Georgia moved swiftly and efficiently to the counter with her cream filling, but her eyes were filled with banked despair. "Do you know what happened to him?" Kat asked quietly.

"Yes. He's married now, with a toddler and another on the way." Georgia switched on the taps and put the double boiler in the sink to soak. She said lightly, "I could have had those urchins. We could have adopted, if I hadn't been so busy seven years ago making decisions for Wynn that I had no business making." She swiped at a counter. "Don't do it, Kathryn."

"Don't what?"

"Don't assume you can make choices for the man you love. You're the one with the problem? That's no big shocker. I always guessed you had a problem.

Most of us have problems unless we've already been canonized. Don't assume he can't handle it." Georgia put her mixture into the refrigerator to cool, then straightened. "Wynn married someone else. I won't. He's there every time I look at another man; he always has been and he always will be, and you are going to New Orleans with Mick."

"Georgia—"

"Sometimes you only get one shot at the brass ring. I blew mine. Damnation, Kathryn. Mick looks at you the way Rhett looked at Scarlett, and if the man asked you to spend the evening in a mud puddle, you'd find four hundred excuses to do it for him. What else is there to say? You're going to New Orleans with him, and that's that!"

Kat saw the tears in Georgia's eyes and walked over with her arms outstretched. Georgia needed the hug— for Wynn, for sharing the kind of secrets only women kept, for being an irreplaceable friend.

Truthfully, though, Georgia didn't understand about Mick. She also didn't know why Mick had asked her to spend the weekend in New Orleans...and yes, she was going.

Mick was counting on New Orleans for a miracle.

Kat was counting on New Orleans for the only possible way and means to end the relationship cleanly and irrevocably. It had to work. She'd stopped believing in miracles a long time ago, and even a miracle couldn't seem to help her stop loving him.

But for the first time in her life, Kat needed help to be strong. And she was counting on that help in New Orleans.

Nine

———

Throughout history, men had done a lot of things to prove their love: climbed mountains, crusaded, fought duels, competed, avenged and revenged.

Mick doubted any of those guys had to go this far. Head bent, he leafed through the magazines in the gynecologist's office. He found a *Woman's World*, *Woman's Day*, *Woman's Life*, and *Woman*, but not a *Sports Illustrated* in the bunch.

Pink vinyl chairs were lined up against one wall. Mick willed his shoulders to shrink, and he squeezed in between a career woman with a swinging ankle and a red-faced housewife. He was the only man in the packed waiting room. Not that he felt out of place, but he was probably the only human being not wearing perfume and waiting for a Pap smear.

Kat had given him the out. "Didn't I agree to go? But there's no reason on earth for you to come to the doctor's office with me."

Technically she was correct. Just as technically, she could have made a doctor's appointment on her own in Charleston—only everyone and his cousin knew Kat at home. No one at home would guess they had anything but a romantic weekend in mind if their destination was New Orleans. More important was the doctor. Not that Mick was fussy on the subject, but he'd nearly had to scout coast-to-coast for someone to fit his qualifications—a woman with a specialty in sexual dysfunction and credentials ten miles long.

"You're not going alone," he'd insisted.

"I don't see why."

He'd touched her cheek. "You don't see why because you're still thinking of this as *your* problem. It's *ours*, Red, and when we have a problem, we handle it together."

Mick figured he was getting good at pontificating. Kat, thankfully, didn't have enough experience with men to recognize one who was desperate.

Twice he'd taken her to the brink of sexual fulfillment. Twice he'd failed her. Something was his fault. He knew it. He felt it enough to have made an appointment with his own doctor, who'd been amused. "After all those years of marriage?" Samuel had murmured. "Teach her to relax, Mick. That's all there is to it, and while you're at it, consider relaxing yourself."

Relax? The doctor hadn't been with her all those hours on the boat, bare and close, where the moon caught every strand of copper in her hair and danced in those soft, vulnerable eyes.

It had taken her a long time to drop her guard and really talk with him. He'd teased her about being Victorian, a judgment that he'd come to understand wasn't fair. Kat wasn't missish. She was proud— fiercely proud and private about infringing on anyone with her problems. She had the insane idea that this dryness was her fault—as if fault had anything to do with intimacy. If he'd left it alone, he knew she planned on never nearing a man's bed again. Much less his.

He wanted her in his life, not just his bed, but the questions were getting a little tricky. How far did a lover's rights extend? Particularly when the lover involved wasn't, precisely, a lover. Particularly when the lady panicked at the first mention of the future. Not surprisingly, when the problem of intimacy was hanging over her head.

But Mick was coming to understand that he had a problem of intimacy hanging over his own head.

Kat needed him. Not for food or shelter or security, and not even—although she saw it as the problem—for sex. Mick understood her particular brand of loneliness because he'd lived it himself. She needed a man she could be honest with, a man who could help her cross those emotional rivers that were tough going alone, a man who'd be there when she wakened from a dark dream in the middle of the night.

Mick needed those same things in return, but he hadn't recognized what he'd been missing until Kat. She was sunshine and warmth and the click of a smile on a gray day. He touched her, and there was the missing half to the whole.

Only Mick needed to know, for himself as well as Kat, that he could come through for her, fill those needs, be that man she could always turn to.

He wouldn't be worried if the situation were your average hurricane, tornado or avalanche. Mick knew what kind of man he was in a crisis, and maybe he was a late starter in this romancing business but catching up wasn't so hard. Lord, the look on her face after he'd sent those camellias!

Maybe a real hero sent camellias, but on a scale of 1 to 10, Mick was willing to bet there wasn't a woman alive who considered being bullied into a gynecologist's visit even remotely romantic. *And what are you gonna do if the doc doesn't find a problem, Larson?*

He didn't know. At the moment, all he knew was that the office was hot, his palms were perspiring and his stomach pitched acid every time he mentally pictured what was going on in the examining room. Before making the appointment, he'd grilled Dr. Krantz on the telephone for more than an hour. She'd reassured him that the examination didn't hurt.

But she didn't know Kat, and maybe it was irrational, but Mick didn't trust anyone physically near Kat but him. She hurt easily, he knew. She was sensitive and she was scared.

He checked his watch for the eighth time. She'd already been in there ten minutes. *Ten minutes.*

In one sense, he wanted the time to race. In another, he'd rather take this torture in slow motion because he knew the toughest time was yet to come. He was increasingly aware that the minutes she spent in that examination office could affect Kat's whole life. But it was how he handled the moment when she came out—

regardless of the doctor's diagnosis—that could affect his. Theirs.

Either he would be the man Kat needed or he would fail her. And as a man, how he wanted to behave and felt he needed to behave for Kat's sake were two entirely different things.

Kat decided that there must be a law regarding doctors' examination rooms. The temperature always seemed to hover around the freezing point. The ceiling tiles always seemed to be pock-marked. And the look of the gloves, glop, and instruments on the counter were designed to make a woman's hands and feet sweat. Copiously.

The door opened, and Kat felt her mouth go dry. The tall woman who strode in had soft gray eyes, flyaway brown hair, and a smile as natural as sunshine. "Kathryn? I'm Maggie Krantz." She extended a hand. "I hope you're as comfortable with first names as I am. Formality never seems to work for me."

"First names are fine," Kat said, and over the next few minutes felt relief gradually slow her hammering pulse. For Mick's sake, she had planned what she was going to say, and whoever stepped through that door didn't make any difference. It helped, though, that the older woman immediately proved easy to talk to. "I know Mick gave you some of my background on the phone, Maggie, but I have to confess that I'm here on false pretenses."

"Oh? I understand you had a problem with dyspareunia." The doctor smiled as she lifted the stethoscope prongs to her ears. When the preliminaries of the exam were finished, she continued, "I know painful intercourse is a touchy subject to talk about, but if you were unaware of this, Kathryn, you're not alone. Very few women escape a bout with the problem at some point during their adult sexual lives. Many times, there's an easily found solution.''

Kat shook her head. ''I need to be honest with you—''

''That's what I'm here for.'' Easily and calmly, Maggie started asking questions, each more intimate and personal than the last. Kat was half surprised to find herself unembarrassed—Mick seemed to have chased that quality out of her character—and she probably answered more thoroughly than the doctor wanted. Her mind wasn't on the questions but on getting back to the subject that mattered. And the first moment Maggie paused, Kat jumped back in.

''I knew before I came here that there was nothing physically wrong with me. Mick knows I have a hard time talking about this, so he thinks I haven't pursued it—not totally, not enough. That isn't true. I have a family doctor at home and an annual exam every year. Five years ago I sought a second opinion. There's just nothing physically wrong.''

''No? Scooch down a little, Kathryn.''

Kat slid, closed her eyes and kept talking. ''Since there was nothing medically wrong, the obvious next stop on the train was psychological. Maybe I haven't taken that far enough, but I went once to a psychologist a long time ago—a total joke. He kept trying to pull some deep fear of sex out of my mental closet, but it just wasn't there. I was never attacked, never abused. My parents are wonderful. I'm not afraid of men. This psychologist said a little hypnosis might help me feel in touch with my real feelings. So we did that."

"And?"

"And he discovered my darkest secret," Kat said dryly. "I'm scared to death of spiders."

"Spiders?" Maggie lifted her head and met Kat's eyes over the sheet. "Me, too." More gently she added, "You're less tense than you were. This'll be done before you know it. Just keep talking, Kathryn."

Kat took a huge breath and did. "What I'm trying to tell you is that I came here for Mick, not for me. I know there's nothing wrong with me, but he needs to think there is. And maybe it isn't medically proper, Maggie, but I'm asking you to invent something. Anything. Right now he's blaming himself for something that's my problem, but he won't listen to me. If you came up with some fancy sounding diagnosis, he'd believe you and he'd stop feeling responsible, and I..."

Her voice dropped off.

Mick thought he'd talked her into this doctor's appointment. That was never true. The truth was she was incapable of walking away from the relationship, and Mick knew it. Mick was under the disastrous impression that she was in love with him—probably because she behaved like she was winsomely, passionately, wildly in love with him every time she was in the same room.

She'd have walked on water for that man. She'd have leaped tall buildings in a single bound because yes, of course she loved him. How could she not? Mick was a heart stealer. He was warm and funny and real, generous in giving, committed, brick-strong and far too perceptive for a woman's peace of mind.

He was also sexy. As hell.

And only a eunuch could have lived with her problems.

"Just about finished, Kathryn."

"Fine," she murmured, but she wasn't. Her heart had never felt so sad. Mick had been trapped in this limbo of a relationship because of her. She couldn't seem to find the strength of character to let him go, and Mick refused to walk away. This doctor's appointment had presented the only solution she could see.

"Maggie, I would pay you. Double your fee or whatever you asked. I don't care what's medically ethical and I don't care. You *have* to tell him that it's me, nothing he could possibly be responsible for."

"No problem." Maggie leaned back and started pulling off her gloves.

Kat felt relief flood through her. "Thank you."

Maggie's smile was dry. "Don't thank me for lying, because I haven't and I won't."

"Pardon?"

"It is you, Kathryn."

Kat jerked up to a sitting position.

"How often have you had a reason to take a prescription for oral antibiotics?" Maggie asked calmly.

"I don't know. Maybe once a year? But I don't see—"

"Why don't you get your clothes on while I take this slide to the lab? And then we'll talk in my office."

Mick saw her the moment she came out. She didn't walk right into the waiting room but stopped at the

receptionist desk, and his so normally graceful Kat
was having a bout of clumsiness. She was fumbling
with her purse, checkbook and pen while she was also
trying to hold on to a small slip of paper that any five
year old could recognize as a prescription form.

The presence of the prescription form told him part
of what he needed to know—the doctor had found
something, an answer. But the look of Kat told him
more. The receptionist was trying to tell her the
amount of the bill. She wasn't listening. Her gaze was
searching the waiting-room crowd for him.

He wasn't hard to spot. He was the one with the
thudding heart, the gray complexion and the slick
hands.

Their eyes met and every bone in his body went soft.
She looked a little dazed, a little disoriented...like
maybe she'd just won the lottery and couldn't believe
it yet. Peach tinted her cheeks under his steady, intense
perusal. He had no doubt whatsoever that she'd forgotten the receptionist, never saw the other waiting
patients. The intimate emotion in her eyes was for
him, only for him. *I can love you, Mick!!!*

But Mick also saw what he'd expected—what he'd
been afraid he would see. There was more than the
celebration of hope in Kat's eyes. There was a new
shyness, a crushing sheen of vulnerability and uncer-
tainty, and Mick thought, *Careful, careful, careful,
Larson.*

She may have won the lottery, but she hadn't spent
the money yet. Obviously that was just occurring to
her.

It had already occurred to him, but for now he
strode toward her. Someone had to save the receptionist who had given up talking and was waving a

hand in Kat's face, trying to get her attention. Kat had dropped her pen, had her checkbook upside down, and the prescription form was about to slip on the floor.

He confiscated the prescription, and within three minutes, neatly steered the bundle of nerves that was Kat out into the New Orleans sunshine.

Nothing was exactly wrong, Kat told herself. At the tail end of August, New Orleans was just as simmering hot as Charleston, but it was cool inside Galatoire's.

The fourth-generation bistro was located on Bourbon Street—their plane didn't leave until morning, so they had the rest of the day and evening to explore Bourbon Street and the French Quarter. Galatoire's couldn't be a better place to start. It was loaded with atmosphere. Mick had already ordered the house specialties: pompano, a jackfish, eggplant stuffed with crabmeat and oysters *en brochette*. He'd backed that up with a liter of bubbling dry champagne. The first glass had already gone straight to her head.

Mick, sitting across from her, had stashed his sport coat. His white shirt complemented his tan and the width of his shoulders. There were other good-looking men in the room. Pip-squeaks. No one had the electrical male charge around him that Mick did; no one else had that slight crook in his lazy grin. He tried to pour her another glass of champagne.

"If I have another one, I'll be weaving instead of walking," she warned him.

"After you eat all that food?"

"I can't possibly eat all this food. You ordered enough for three."

"I've seen your appetite before, Red. You'll have this polished off while I'm still on the first course."

See, she kept telling herself. Nothing was wrong. Mick was teasing her just like he always teased her, smiling like he always smiled, and he was relaxed in a way that usually gave her enormous pleasure that he could relax around her. He just hadn't mentioned the doctor.

Somehow she'd been quite positive that he'd be in a rush to hear the doctor's news.

On the cab drive through the city, she hadn't known quite what to say or how to say it. Now, though, she felt abruptly impatient with herself. If there was a human being alive she could discuss anything with, it was Mick—he'd taught her that, and maybe it was past time she proved that his lessons had gotten through. "The problem," she mentioned casually, "is called *Candida Albicans*."

His gaze was riveted on her face, but only for a moment. His grin was lazy and slow. "Sounds like a Mexican breed of jumping bean."

She ducked her head to spear a bite of jackfish. "Actually it's nothing more than a common yeast infection. Nothing serious, nothing awful. There's no reason to think seven days on medication won't take care of it—although Maggie suggested I follow up with my own doctor, given my own particular history." She was still having trouble believing it. Seven days to erase a problem that she'd spent years building into an unbridgeable emotional trauma. She wasn't inadequate. She wasn't half a woman.

And the man who'd made sure she found that out calmly split a roll in half and handed her the buttered wedge. "If it's all that common—"

"It's common, but Maggie said it can be very hard to diagnose. Many women have clear-cut symptoms; I never did. At least, nothing I understood was a symptom." She shifted restlessly in her seat. Mick was listening, but he wasn't asking any questions. She could have let it go right there, if she hadn't learned to demand real honesty—from herself and for him.

"I never lied to my family doctor, Mick. I just didn't realize that there were certain things I should have told him. I didn't know there could be a link between broad spectrum antibiotics and yeast infections. I didn't realize that a yeast infection could be a reason why a woman felt pain when she was making love. And the one physical symptom I had..." Kat hesitated. It's not that she wasn't willing to tell him, but "itches" were hardly conversational material around a gourmet lunch. "I never understood it was a symptom; I just assumed it was a problem that all women had. Being fussy about personal hygiene has always been second nature to me, and other than that I never thought about it."

Mick lifted a bite of eggplant, silently asking her if she wanted to try it. Kat shook her head, becoming more confused by the minute. Mick was as relaxed as if they were discussing the weather.

"Maggie said that it happens all the time. Women are very good at ignoring physical symptoms, especially if they think their real problem is sexual. Bring in sexuality, and their first impulse is to believe it's their fault, something they're doing wrong, something they're lacking."

When Mick saw she was finished, he signaled for the waiter. "Women don't have a corner on that market, Red. Men are just as good at setting that scene themselves. Beds can be an emotional land mine for both sexes."

"Yes," she said vaguely. When he'd set his napkin down, his fingers had brushed hers and immediately withdrawn. Sort of like his hand had come in contact with a hot potato.

He smiled at her when they rose from the table, and he guided her through the restaurant with a hand at the small of her back. His hand, however, never quite touched.

They heard hours of wonderful music that night. The down and gutsy jazz New Orleans was famous for, rock coming out of neon-flashing nightclubs, the ancient and enduring lovesongs from a place with candlelight and dark corners—Bourbon Street had it all. At two in the morning they were still strolling the streets, stuffed on Creole cooking and champagne, high on music and the lights of a city created for lovers. And in smiles, in quietly shared looks, in everything he said, Mick made her feel like the most cherished of all lovers.

But when they reached the hotel, he simply fitted her key into the adjoining door next to his. His knuckles brushed her cheek but he didn't kiss her. Didn't even try. "Sleep well, sweetheart."

Alone in the hotel bedroom, Kat started tugging off clothes. She told herself that it was perfectly natural that he was keeping a physical distance. For one thing she was out of commission, so to speak, for at least the next seven days. And for another, she'd put Mick through some heavy tease and torture from the very beginning of the relationship. He undoubtedly didn't want to start something that couldn't be finished, and she'd commit hara-kiri before putting him through that again.

Only not kissing or touching her was unlike Mick. He was physical, had always been physical. He touched as naturally as he breathed. He'd kissed her a hundred times when it wasn't wise. For that matter Kat couldn't remember a single time when Mick had had her alone that he'd cared chicken scratch for wisdom.

She slipped in between the cool sheets and fluffed the pillow. *Kat, that man has invested one heck of a lot of grief in you. He would hardly be likely to turn cool now, when there's finally a chance of a future.*

Unless, of course, that had hit Mick. They had a chance of a future now, and perhaps that possibility had hit him like a binding noose. He hadn't been that happy with June. He hadn't been that unhappy single, and she'd hardly been God's gift to a man's life. Mick had needs. Their whole relationship had been dominated by hers.

"Of course we had a good time with Uncle Bill. We always have a good time with Uncle Bill." Noel, sitting in the back seat with Angie, hadn't gotten her father's attention since they were picked up. "Unlike you, Dad, he lets us stay up to all hours and eat anything we want."

"Mmmm."

She tried one more time. "We also saw an R-rated movie. Lots of violence, lots of sex."

"Hmmm."

Noel shared a glance with Angie. Angie shrugged. "You two had a good time in New Orleans, right?"

"Wonderful," Kat murmured.

"Terrific," Mick concurred.

The radio was on. A male tenor was making a tragedy out of "It Had To Be You." The sun had been blinding bright from the moment they'd stepped off the plane; tiredness had seeped into Kat's soul and Mick's thigh was inches from hers. All day, there'd been a thousand chances for that thigh or his hand to touch hers.

Noel suddenly swung over the front seat. "Uh, Dad?"

"Hmmm?"

"Funeral homes probably have a hot line to that radio station. You don't mind if I find something peppier, do you?"

"It Had To Be You" was instantly replaced by an ancient beat about a guy who couldn't get no satisfaction. Mick switched off the radio so fast that Kat felt her cheeks burn.

"You know it's the first of September tomorrow, don't you? That means school," Angie groaned. "It's not fair. It's still too hot to go to school, and besides that it's my birthday next week. Nobody should have to go to school on their birthday, should they, Kat?"

"No way," Kat agreed. Two days ago Mick would have teasingly called her a traitor for siding with his daughters. Now he gave her a vague smile, like the kind he'd give a wayward sister.

Coming home, Kat had been worried how the girls would take their weekend. Mick argued with her that it was a healthy thing for any kid to understand that adults occasionally needed time alone, and nothing else had to be said. She could see he was right. Maybe the girls were curious, but they were hardly stressed out about it, which meant that being around his daughters was hardly a reason for Mick's increasing distance.

"I invited a few friends to spend the night next Friday rather than have a birthday party this year. That's okay with you, isn't it, Dad?"

Mick stared at his youngest in the rearview mirror. "How many is a few?"

Noel, suspiciously smoother than oil, piped in before Angie had to answer. "I'm going to die if I don't eat soon. How much farther until we get home?"

"Another fifteen minutes."

"What are we going to have for dinner?"

"The first thing I find in the freezer that'll defrost at the speed of sound. I think the larder's down to either liver or meat loaf."

Both girls groaned, but more than that Kat heard the weariness in Mick's voice. Again, she was conscious of how often her needs had dominated their relationship and she automatically responded. "Your dad's tired. Why don't you all come over to my place? I know I have some fries, and it wouldn't take very long to whip up a salad and put some chops on the grill."

"That's a great idea, Kat! Then you can help me decide what to wear to school tomorrow."

"And I want to talk to you about my pajama party."

Mick interjected, "Kat has to unpack and she's just as tired as I am. The last thing she needs to do is put on a dinner for four."

"Honestly, I don't mind. I already have everything around, so it's no trouble," Kat promised him.

"So let's do it, Dad! It's okay with you, isn't it?"

Stopped at a red light, Mick turned his head. The look in his eyes was as warm as love, as intense as a flame. She didn't belong to him, but with him. The hunger in his gaze was so real she could have reached out and touched it, but then it was gone. As carefully as a man dealing with dynamite, he said quietly, "We'll come, but only if you're sure that's what you want, Kathryn."

If you're sure that's what you want, Kathryn?

Mick hadn't been that courteous when he'd been married and they'd been mildly acquainted neighbors.

Kat was briefly tempted to shake his big shoulders good and hard. She might have done that if she hadn't been feeling more and more despairing. Mick was emotionally closing off from her and she had no idea why.

Ten

The following Thursday night, Kat walked in her door at nine o'clock after a tennis game with the three Larsons next door. The game had been hilarious. Mick was the only one who could play; the three females had done nothing but chase balls. All four of them had laughed, including Kat, but she wasn't laughing as she headed for the shower.

If Mick was trying to totally destroy her sanity, he was doing an excellent job of it.

Tonight it had been tennis. The night before she'd had to work late, and the whole crew had shown up with fast food so she wouldn't have to cook. Tuesday Mick had asked her to shop for Angie's birthday present, and Monday they'd all piled into the car for a trip to the grocery store.

Nothing was wrong with any of those outings, and certainly none of them were contrived. Each, though, had reminded Kat of how inexorably the two house-holds had been merging for some time. The girls had long had a key to her place. Kat's favorite brand of tea was in Nick's cupboard; his Allen wrench was in her drawer; and the girls' clutter of shoes and tapes and forgotten sweaters was as much in evidence in her house as his.

Such togetherness was perfectly natural when the two adults involved were about to form a permanent alliance. Judging from the amount of togetherness Mick had pushed this week—she hadn't had a free minute to herself—Kat could hardly doubt he had marriage in mind. A dozen times she'd told herself that nothing had changed, but it had. Oh, God, it had.

Suddenly Mick had developed the manners of a knight, the camaraderie of a girl's best friend, and the trustworthy dependability of a Boy Scout.

He just stayed as physically and emotionally far away from her as if she'd recently contracted a lethal case of cooties.

By midnight, she still couldn't seem to sit, settle, or sleep. Carrying a glass of cooking sherry, she opened her bedroom's French doors and settled on the wrought-iron balcony. The household next door was dark, and it was a good night for an insomniac's brood. The air was sultry and still, darker than secrets and redolent with the scents of late roses and honey-suckle. Even a hardened cynic could turn romantic on a night like this.

Miserable, Kat gulped another dreadful swig of sherry.

"Hi, Red."

Startled, she looked up to Mick's third story. With the lights off behind him, she could just make out his shadowed form straddling the windowsill. Heaven knew how long he'd been there.

"Couldn't sleep?"

"No," she murmured, unaware until that moment that he had a clear view into her bedroom, wondering how often she'd undressed with the light on behind sheer lace curtains.

"Often, honey."

"Pardon?"

He talked for a while. About what, she had no idea. What mattered was that he wanted to talk, and the hunger in his voice carried in the darkness like a call to her senses. She was only dressed in a nightgown. There hadn't been any reason to put on a robe. It was hot, it was dark, it was past midnight. He couldn't see her, no one could see her, but she felt the intensity of his eyes on hers. She felt his voice like the touch of skin. She felt Mick. Lonesome and alone in his third-story bedroom.

And chitchat suddenly wasn't going to cut it. "Mick," she said quietly, "if there's something on your mind, I wish you'd say it."

"Something on my mind?"

She took a breath. "If there's something bothering you, something you want to talk to me about . . ."

He hesitated. "There is something."

She could feel herself bracing for the blow. This was it. The reason he had been withdrawing from her. Mick had changed her whole world, though, and Kat promised herself she would do her best to be understanding and supportive, no matter how much it hurt.

"I'm real confused about putting together this quarter's tax forms. You fill out the same small independent business forms that I do, don't you?"

It took a moment for her vocal chords to function. "Taxes? You want to talk about taxes?"

He did, productively and enlighteningly, until nearly two in the morning. Twice Kat opened her mouth to interject a change of subject, but in the end simply couldn't. How, after all, could a woman possibly ask a man why he'd lost total interest in sending her camellias?

Exhaustion caught up with her by Friday. She'd fallen asleep on the couch when the phone, most unkindly, jangled at eleven.

"I'm in trouble, Red."

If he'd meant it, she would have jumped. If he'd needed her, she was dying to jump, but the way he rolled "Red" off his tongue lacked any trace of seriousness. Kat couldn't take anymore, not tonight.

"Mick," she said softly, "Don't."

"Don't what?"

"Don't play it like this. If this is your way of letting me down easy by playing it like friends, I'd just rather—"

"I have no idea what you're talking about, but this is no time to dither. I have a crisis situation here."

"Sure, you do."

Aggravation seeped through his voice. "There are thirteen girls downstairs. I was banished to the third floor from the time they all got in pajamas."

"I'm not coming over there," she said firmly.

"I thought they'd go to sleep. They're never going to sleep. You have no idea what my living room looks like. Lord, I just heard a lamp crash."

"Mick—"

"They keep screaming. For God's sake, Red. I can't handle this alone."

It sounded as shaky as a used-car salesman's line, but there was, after all, the thousand to one chance Mick actually had his hands full. Kat pulled on jeans and a blouse and arrived next door within five minutes, only to discover that thirteen girls having a pajama party said it all. She stayed downstairs long enough to share a pop and potato chips and to meet Angie's friends. Then, most reluctantly, she went in search of Mick.

She found him at the top of his third-floor stairs, hunched over with his elbows on his knees, and suddenly the whole situation wasn't as easy to read as she'd assumed. Maybe he'd trumped up a silly excuse to get her over here, but the shadows under his eyes were as dark as hers and the tension in his shoulders was real.

"Could you reason with them?"

"Mick, you don't reason with girls at a pajama party."

"They shriek every time I go downstairs. Even my own daughter."

"Shrieking at pajama parties is the status quo. So is renting horror movies and staying up all night."

"Did you see their faces?"

"They've been experimenting with makeup. That's status quo, too."

"Not for Angie. Angie doesn't like makeup and she can't stand boys, but do you know what they've been talking about nonstop for the past three hours?"

"Boys," Kat said dryly.

"Do you have any idea how much pop thirteen girls can take in?"

"Yes," she said calmly.

"Ten pizzas. Thirteen girls. They're pigs."

"Yes," she said calmly.

"It's no wonder they have to yell. Every appliance is on in the place, TVs, VCR, radios, tape player. Don't try to tell me that's natural."

"Mick, they're having a perfectly wonderful time."

He murmured, "Yeah. I know."

His voice was barely a murmur, but the humor was punctuated by the kneading pressure of his thumbs somewhere in the neighborhood of her left shoulder blade. She remembered sitting on the step below him, but not the precise moment he'd shifted her between the scissor of his legs.

She was either a sucker for a back rub or a sucker for Mick. Probably both. Especially since he hadn't come this close in nearly a week. "You're so tense, so tired, Red. And you think I like those circles under your eyes?"

The stairwell was shadowed and he wasn't making much sense. For a brief time she didn't care. He gently pushed her head down and used his fingertips to give her a scalp rub. She closed her eyes and felt muscle after muscle liquify. His thumbs and palms pummeled and soothed, not a prelude-to-lovemaking kind of back rub but a more intimate kind. He knew her body. He knew where every nerve was strained, every muscle was knotted.

"Talking purely theoretically, you're going to make a rotten stepmother, Kathryn," he murmured absently.

"Hmmm?"

"Not on their terms, just on mine. Your concept of discipline is zip and you're never going to back me up." He sounded amused. "You side with every damn thing they do. You understand every damn thing they do. And I'm telling you right now, Red, I don't want you to change. We'll probably fight, but that's okay. Stay the way you are, and...hey, where're you going?"

Maybe every tendon in her body had turned into noodles, but her weight miraculously held when she stood up. *"Home."* Either his back rub or his "theoretical" discussion of stepmothers had brought on an instant attack of the blues.

"Honey, turn around and look at me."

She didn't. His voice was as smooth as melted butter, and like a fool, she felt dampness coat her lashes. She headed down the stairs. Quickly.

"It's not what you think, Kat. Try to remember we were friends long before we tried to be lovers."

She remembered that for the next week. It didn't help. Mick might want to return their relationship back to friends, but that wasn't the emotion she felt for him and it never would be.

Alone in her house the following Wednesday night, she took a long warm shower guaranteed to relax her. It didn't. Afterward, she paced the house in her towel. She circled her carousel horse, tracked the length of the hall, then stalked upstairs. Pausing by her bedroom window, she saw lightning slash a zigzag of silver against the night sky. She saw...but not really.

Until midday yesterday, she'd clung to the hope that there was an obvious reason for Mick's change in behavior. Although her prescription had run out after seven days, she hadn't been able to schedule the follow-up visit with her doctor until yesterday. Conceivably Mick had deliberately avoided any physical contact until she had the doctor's okay. Last night, though, she'd managed to slip in an "I'm fine" over a tuna noodle casserole dinner with him and the girls, and Mick hadn't blinked an eye. More relevant, lots and lots of hours had passed between last night and tonight.

The hurt was starting to feel as sharp and real as a knife wound.

He cared. Kat couldn't possibly doubt that. He'd pursued her with exhausting single-minded determination. He spent every moment of his free time with her. Kat had always known she wasn't prize stepmom material, but she loved Angie and Noel. The reverse was just as true, and Mick was the one who'd pushed for an even deeper relationship with his daughters.

What mattered even more to Kat was that Mick had changed. Couldn't he see it? Work was no longer his life. He still made a big deal out of every crisis with Noel and Angie but that was nonsense; he was a terrific father—at least he was now that he'd let himself open up and just be with them. He'd just needed someone to tell him that was okay. Someone who could make him laugh, someone he didn't have to feel on with, someone who accepted him for the man he was...and wanted to be.

Kat had so fiercely believed she was part of those changes in Mick. She'd thought he was growing, changing in ways he wanted to grow and change. She'd thought...maybe...that he was capturing something with her that really mattered to him.

She'd thought that he loved her.

Kat shoved her shower-damp hair back from her scalp. The ache of loss would tear her apart if she let it. Anger was the easier emotion to deal with, and she certainly felt that, too.

Didn't she have a reason? He'd taken her halfway to the moon and then pitched the mission. He'd made her want, ravenously, and then shut it off. He'd forced her to talk about dreadful things, face up to mortifying and embarrassing things, dragged her to that doctor and made the whole damn thing seem natural between a man and a woman who loved each other. And then dropped her back to the status of friends.

Kat would have tried to accept that if it just made sense, but it didn't. Mick would never deliberately hurt her, would never leave any woman hanging. He had a mischievous side, but he was an honest and straightforward man. If he'd stopped loving her, he would have cut the relationship off cleanly.

And the only exception that Kat could think of was if Mick had barreled in something he couldn't be honest about...couldn't handle...at least not alone.

Heaven knew, Kat understood the dimensions of that kind of problem, and she had paced halfway to her bedroom when that particular mental light bulb switched on. The wattage started at dim and gradually accelerated to illuminating brightness. Damn, she thought.

Abruptly she dropped her towel, shimmied into a robe, strode into the study and punched the buttons on the telephone on her desk. The phone rang once. Then again and again. Mick picked it up halfway through the fourth ring. He'd obviously been asleep, because his voice was groggy and scratchy.

Hers was belligerent. "I need your help, Larson. I have a leaky faucet."

There was a brief hesitation. "Now?"

"Now."

"Sweetheart, it's almost midnight."

"The faucet is very leaky."

"We're talking flood?"

"You bet your sweet patooties we're talking flood."

"Okay, honey. I'll be there."

He hung up, and Kat felt her whole body turn shivery. Would he misunderstand all that drivel? She hoped not. Mick might have taught her that honest communication was the key to a relationship... but he'd also taught her that a light touch worked best when the subject was sticky.

Problems didn't get any stickier than this, and she swiftly glanced at a clock. It wouldn't take him three minutes to tug on a pair of jeans. That left her barely enough time to fix the sash on her robe, take a brush to her hair and race downstairs to answer his knock.

Thunder growled, close and ominously, as she opened the back door. Mick stepped into her kitchen wearing a sweatshirt and jeans and carrying a tool kit. He took one long look at her and smiled. Slowly. "So... where's the leak, Red?"

"The upstairs bathroom."

"Ah."

She climbed the stairs ahead of him. He set the tool kit down on the bathroom floor and surveyed her spotless black marble sink with a grave expression. "Looks pretty serious."

"I know."

"I'm pretty handy, but I'm afraid this is bad enough for a qualified plumber."

"I was afraid of that."

"You know where the pipes under the sink go?"

"In there."

"In where?"

She motioned vaguely. "In there."

He didn't take the tool kit into her bedroom, just strode in ahead of her and paused, taking in the sleigh bed, the Victorian hatboxes, the bottles of scents on her dresser, the fireplace and stained-glass windows. "Can't see a single pipe," he mentioned.

"You sure?"

"I'm sure. Maybe if you'd turn off that overhead, I could see better."

She turned off the glaring overhead light, which left only the soft-prismed glass lamp burning behind her bed. "Better now?"

He didn't answer the question. His focus honed with hopeless intensity on her short silk robe, her tousled hair, her mouth. Especially her mouth. Lord, was his tongue suddenly dry. "The leaky pipes were fun...but I'm through with that anytime you are. You're obviously on to me, Red."

"Heaven knows why it took me so long, but yes."

"I don't want you scared. I never wanted you scared."

"And that's what these past two weeks have been about, wasn't it?" Gently she closed the bedroom door. "For the first time in my life I could make love—and that was wonderful, Mick, only you knew I'd suddenly realize that was the first time. The first time that mattered." Her fingers unwrapped the sash of her robe. "There's no way on earth I would marry a man I couldn't satisfy in bed. I wouldn't do that to me, and I'd never, never, *never* have done that to you."

"Honey—"

He stopped talking when she pushed the robe off her right shoulder, then her left. Gravity did the rest; it whooshed to the floor. Mick wasn't seeing anything he hadn't seen before, but the emotion in his eyes was new. Hunger, yearning, desire, need—she'd seen those in him before...but not anxiety. Never before anxiety.

"Given the time to worry about it," she said softly, "I would have built that 'first time' into a test...such a critical test that I'd be tense as a wire—a sure guarantee it would go badly. You knew that, didn't you, Mick? So you made very sure I had no time to worry about it. You told me in a hundred ways over the past two weeks that sex was absolutely no priority for you."

His voice hoarsened, deepened, when he saw her walking toward him. "Sex isn't a priority. Love is, and I mean that from the heart, Kat. We don't have to do this, not tonight, not if you don't—"

She latched her arms around his neck and effectively silenced him with a kiss. Mick was sensitive and perceptive and wonderful, but just this time he was dead wrong. They did have to do this, and there was no way around it being a terribly critical test. Kat had always understood what the stakes might be the first time they consummated their love—she could lose him.

She was physically and emotionally incapable of not being afraid of tonight...but at this precise moment she was less afraid than she could be, might be, probably should be. Mick had walked in the door with a slow smile, but she'd also glimpsed the stark anxiety in his eyes.

Mick was the only man she knew who understood the terribly fragile, mortifyingly private fears in a woman's heart. How could she have failed to realize that he had buried fears of his own? In a few minutes she would undoubtedly remember to be afraid again, but right now she had a man to take care of. With alluring softness, with the power of a woman's soul, she kissed him until his arms swept around her and his hands were clutching her hair.

Still, he tore his mouth free from hers. "Honey, if you're not absolutely sure—"

She pushed. He fell. The sleigh bed had high sloping sides, a feather bed mattress, a dozen pillows. Sprawled, Mick looked as much at home as a lumberjack in a perfumery. Crystal lamplight twinkled on his slow male smile.

"Your whole bedroom's pure woman. No surprise." His thumb rubbed the line of her cheekbone, his gaze never wavering from her face. "I'm getting the feeling that you're in the mood, Red. Like to hell with the tests."

"Larson, I've been waiting thirty-three years. Not for this, but for you. I'm dying and you want to talk?"

"I'm just trying to understand. What happened to the worry? What happened to my Victorian lady of the corsets and cameos? Where are all those inhibitions I know so well?"

His teasing made her smile, but not for long. His pulse was erratic, his heartbeat thudding, and his eyes had the sheen of desire, but the anxiety was still there. Mick didn't want her to know that he'd made his own test out tonight. He was just as afraid as she was. She'd guessed that he was afraid of physically hurting her, and even more of failing her as a lover and a man.

Kat knelt beside him. The only man she would ever love had a problem: a problem so private, so vulnerable, that he assumed he couldn't share it.

Those were the problems that lovers shared best. Mick had taught her that, but if he didn't know it applied to him, he would. Soon. Slower than slow motion she pushed up his sweatshirt and let her palms glide sensually over his warm, bare skin. He eased up to a sitting position only long enough to drag it off, but when he reached for her she shook her head.

"I've worried so much about this," she whispered, "and all for the wrong reasons." Her fingers walked down his ribs to the snap of his jeans. She nudged the snap, then met his eyes as she slid down the zipper. "I built up fear, and for what? We've never failed at anything that mattered, because we've never failed each other. Love's continued to grow—not in spite of, but because of what we've shared together, so how can I be afraid of loving you? I'm not. I'm not even afraid of telling you how desperately and brazenly I want you...."

Her palms slipped inside his waistband. His jeans wanted to stick to him like a jealous woman. Kat wasn't tolerating any rivals, not tonight. She tugged and pulled the denim, well aware that Mick had heard her because slowly his eyes darkened, softened, blurred. He wasn't breathing as well as he had been. His body temperature was rising, and it wasn't anxiety tautening his muscles now.

Kat, though, wasn't through. "I've had dreams about you," she whispered. "All through this heat wave, I've had a recurring dream about you...and the heat...in a storm." She had to get up to pull his jeans off. On the way back, her fingers skimmed against the grain of his hair, over knees, then thighs. When she reached his white cotton underwear, she took a long, wanton look at him. He liked that look. His response was so elemental that she had to continue. "They weren't nice dreams, Mick. They were dark and erotic and wild. I dreamed about making love with you, outside in a storm, with the rain coming down on a hot, windy midnight, and you bare. Just as bare as you are now, and I ache in that dream. Shamelessly. You're so hard and powerful when you move between my thighs and suddenly you're riding me. The rain keeps coming and your skin is all hot and wet and slick—"

"I hope you're through talking, Red, because if you don't cut it out you're going to see a hair-trigger problem like most boys outgrow by fourteen."

She heard the end-of-a-tether growl in his voice. She smiled soothingly...and dropped his briefs off the end of the bed.

He swore, very low, very softly—maybe softer than she'd ever heard him swear—and then reached for her. Somewhere, thunder rumbled. The curtains billowed with a sudden burst of cool air, but Kat barely noticed. She found herself abruptly sandwiched between perfume-scented sheets and Mick—a towering, tense and primitively male Mick.

She couldn't see a single trace of anxiety. He'd also lost all interest in talking, and his first kiss singed and sizzled all the way to her belly. He wreaked further devastation with the second, and then his tongue claimed hers, sweeping the dark warmth of her mouth, sipping the moisture from her. He raised himself to cup one pearl-white breast, rubbing the tip until it swelled, then letting his tongue cool the surface until it throbbed.

Kat had wanted him to feel so wanted and desired that he would forget any fears that it wouldn't go well. She'd forgotten that he was a master of the same game. Lamplight washed his features golden and hard. He kissed her everywhere, anywhere, until her flesh shimmered and her bones turned liquid. His hands were magical, his mouth dangerous, and he played on the one fear she hadn't known existed. She was going to die soon, if he didn't take her.

Lord, she loved him.

Outside, lightning lit up the black sky. A giant roar of thunder made the bedside lamp blink, then grow dark. With the darkness came rain, but Mick didn't care. Kat was coming apart, for him...with him. She'd come to him in passion before, but never with a need so seeped in love that the two were inseparable.

Her legs twisted around him when he stroked her soft core. The deeper he probed, the more ember-hot her kisses became...and the more satiny moisture he found. He clawed the air on the side of the bed for his jeans.

"No," she whispered fiercely. "We don't need it." She gently bit his shoulder, skimmed her hands down his sides to his hips. "Wouldn't you like a son, Mick?"

Love rushed through him to the beat and spatter of rain.

"I love you," she whispered.

He'd known, but she'd never said it. He couldn't seem to breathe. He couldn't seem to stop his heart from swelling.

And then she whispered, "Come to me."

Kat opened her arms, beckoning. She kissed his face, his throat, his mouth—dozens of impatient kisses—as he shifted over her and wrapped her legs around him. He lifted her hips and it began, the slow snug intrusion, the sensation of being impaled and a part of—irreversibly a part of—the man she loved. Mick didn't move then, didn't dare breathe.

In the darkness he saw her lashes lift and her luminous eyes meet his. Her arms and thighs tightened at the same time. "Don't you dare ask me how good this feels," she murmured.

He didn't have to. He could see. He could feel, and he gave her a fantasy ride of making love in a midnight wind with the rain pouring down, hurling toward ecstasy in a heat wave created solely by two. He gave her pleasure, as she'd only dreamed of it . . . but she made him love, as he hadn't known was possible.

"I'm back!"

"So I see," Mick murmured humorously. She had stayed cuddled in his arms for a long, languid and loving half hour. Knowing Kat, he should have known that peacefulness wouldn't last. She'd sprung up with the electric excitement of a new millionairess. The storm was still raging. She'd jumped up to close the windows and then raced downstairs to bring up candles.

Finally she was back where he wanted her, straddling him with her long white limbs, stroking close. The flickering candles illuminated the indefatigably sassy glint in her eyes. Her shoulders had a provocative tilt. Her mouth had a saucy curve. Conceivably, just conceivably, the lady had just discovered that without a doubt she could make love—real love, wonderful, unforgettable love.

Mick had never seen her higher, but he planned to. Over the next sixty years, he had a lot of plans for Kat.

"Am I cutting off your circulation?"

"Only when you squirm." Which, he was well aware, she was doing deliberately. He couldn't seem to stop smiling. He pushed a strand of hair behind her ear.

"Mick?"

"Hmmm?"

"I'm unbearably happy."

"You just think you are. You still have miles to go before you ever catch up with me." Her brow needed a kiss. "The girls are going to think I'm going to marry you. Particularly if I call them at six in the morning for the express purpose of telling them that."

"Good heavens. Was that a proposal?"

He shook his head. "No way. Tonight we'll order some moonlight and maybe a gremlin will pop for camellias. We'll have a little dinner, a little champagne. Then, maybe you'll get a proposal. I'm not promising. You'll just have to worry until then whether my intentions are honorable."

She shifted her legs in a way that made him groan, and her smile. Honorable intentions were not on her mind. "You liked that idea of a son."

"Our son? Yes, love."

"It'll undoubtedly be a daughter."

"I'm prepared for that. The odds are already against me. One more female couldn't possibly make my life more difficult."

"Mick..." She brushed his eyebrows with the pads of her thumbs, but she was suddenly serious. "From the moment I walked into your backyard, you've made my life terribly difficult. So difficult that I don't know what would have happened to me... if it hadn't been you. Just you. Have you ever tasted despair?''

He said gently, ''Oh, sweetheart. I definitely tasted yours.''

''I thought it was me and I thought it was hopeless and I'd given up.''

He combed both hands through her hair, making a tangled mess, but at least it held her head still. Blue eyes met tobacco brown. Neither even tried to look away. ''You'd only given up, honey, because you hadn't been in love before. Not in love the right way. If it's the right way, honesty becomes second nature. If it's the right way, being vulnerable isn't scary because both people are looking to protect each other's needs. And Kat?''

''Hmmm?''

He said softly, ''You weren't the only one who needed that lesson. I needed to know—as much as you did—that I could tell you when I was afraid. Afraid as a man. Afraid as a lover.''

She kissed him. A reward for owning up that he'd been afraid. She had some work to do with Mick before he really believed he could equally come to her with a need, any need. She'd be there. He knew that now, but he'd know it even better after fifty or sixty years together. She kissed him again. Hard and thoroughly.

''Lord, you're in the mood again,'' he murmured.

''Yes.''

''How much can a man be expected to handle?''

''I don't know about most men.'' She kissed him again. ''I just know about you. There isn't anything you can't handle, Mick. There also isn't anything you haven't. Not where I'm concerned."

"It's past two..."

"Poor baby," she said sympathetically.

"Minute by minute," he said delicately, "you're getting more brazen, more bold, more wanton."

"Yes."

"Your hands are in the cookie jar again, Red. You like trouble."

"Yes."

What could he do? He twisted her around and slowly down, and before her spine reached the sheets her arms were around him.

* * * * *

SILHOUETTE® Desire™

COMING NEXT MONTH

#559 SUNSHINE—Jo Ann Algermissen
A Florida alligator farm? It was just what ad exec Rob Emery *didn't* need! But sharing the place with Angelica Franklin made life with the large lizards oh, so appealing....

#560 GUILTY SECRETS—Laura Leone
Leah McCargar sensed sexy houseguest Adam Jordan was not *all* he claimed. But before she could prove him guilty of lying, she became guilty... of love.

#561 THE HIDDEN PEARL—Celeste Hamilton
Aunt Eugenia's final match may be her toughest! Can Jonah Pendleton coax shy Maggie O'Grady into leading a life of adventure? The next book in the series *Aunt Eugenia's Treasures.*

#562 LADIES' MAN—Raye Morgan
Sensible Trish Becker knew that Mason Ames was nothing more than a good-looking womanizer! But she still couldn't stop herself from succumbing to his seductive charms.

#563 KING OF THE MOUNTAIN—Joyce Thies
Years ago Gloria Hubbard had learned that rough, tough William McCann was one untamable man. Now he was back in town... and back in her life.

#564 SCANDAL'S CHILD—Ann Major
When May's *Man of the Month* Officer Garret Cagan once again saved scandalous Noelle Martin from trouble, the Louisiana bayou wasn't the only thing steaming them up....

AVAILABLE NOW:

#553 HEAT WAVE
Jennifer Greene

#554 PRIVATE PRACTICE
Leslie Davis Guccione

#555 MATCHMAKER, MATCHMAKER
Donna Carlisle

#556 MONTANA MAN
Jessica Barkley

#557 THE PASSIONATE ACCOUNTANT
Sally Goldenbaum

#558 RULE BREAKER
Barbara Boswell

AVAILABLE NOW—

the books you've been waiting for by one of
America's top romance authors!

DIANA PALMER
DUETS

Ten years ago Diana Palmer published her very fir
romances. Powerful and dramatic, these gripping tal
of love are everything you have come to expect fro
Diana Palmer.

This month some of these titles are available again
DIANA PALMER DUETS—a special three-book colle
tion. Each book has two wonderful stories plus an intr
duction by the author. You won't want to miss them!

Book 1
SWEET ENEMY
LOVE ON TRIAL

Book 2
STORM OVER THE LAKE
TO LOVE AND CHERISH

Book 3
IF WINTER COMES
NOW AND FOREVER

Available now at your favorite retail outlet.

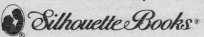
Silhouette Books ®

A celebration of motherhood by three of your favorite authors!

JENNIFER GREENE
KAREN KEAST
EMILIE RICHARDS

This May, expect something wonderful from Silhouette Books — BIRDS, BEES AND BABIES — a collection of three heartwarming stories bundled into one very special book.

It's a lullaby of love . . . dedicated to the romance of motherhood.

Look for BIRDS, BEES AND BABIES in May at your favorite retail outlet.

BBB-1